BODY DOUBLE

PRAISE FOR **Body Double**

"Spare, poetic, and endlessly enticing, this windy tale of obsession had me hooked and spooked. *Single White Female* with a chicly bleak Scandinavian sensibility."
—Brittany Newell, author of *Soft Core*

"A razor-sharp novel of exquisite prose and uncanny tension, *Body Double* lures the unsuspecting reader into a sophisticated hall of mirrors where obsession blurs the lines between self and other. Bravo!"
—Antoine Wilson, author of *Mouth to Mouth*

PRAISE FOR **Antiquity**

"While Johansson is as mordant and hypnotic as Nabokov, she opts for restraint over pyrotechnics. (Credit is also due to Kira Josefsson's deft translation from the Swedish.) This is a novel to savor and argue with . . . I've come to think of *Antiquity* as a Polaroid of the ocean at night, a deep-time abyss, an intimate menace."
—RYAN CHAPMAN, *The New York Times Book Review*

"One exquisitely rendered moment after another . . . *Antiquity* maps out the crystallizing process of an impression, the places in a temporary affair where the fleshy stuff of love or lust hardens into narrative."
—ROSA BOSHIER GONZÁLEZ, *The Believer*

BODY DOUBLE

A NOVEL

Hanna Johansson

Translated by Kira Josefsson

SCRIBE
Melbourne | London | Minneapolis

Scribe Publications
18–20 Edward St, Brunswick, Victoria 3056, Australia
2 John St, Clerkenwell, London, WC1N 2ES, United Kingdom
3754 Pleasant Ave, Suite 223w, Minneapolis, Minnesota 55409, USA

First published by Norstedts, Sweden
Published by arrangement with Nordin Agency AB, Sweden
Published by Scribe 2026

Copyright © Hanna Johansson 2026
Translation copyright © Kira Josefsson 2026

All rights reserved. The publisher expressly prohibits the use of this book in connection with the development of any software program, including, without limitation, training a machine-learning or generative artificial intelligence (AI) system. Without limiting the rights under copyright reserved above, no part of this publication may be reproduced, stored in or introduced into a retrieval system, or transmitted, in any form or by any means without the prior written permission of the publisher.

The moral rights of the author and translator have been asserted.

This is a work of fiction. All the characters, organisations, and events portrayed in this novel are either products of the author's imagination or used fictitiously.

Text design by tracy danes

Printed and bound in the UK by CPI Group (UK) Ltd, Croydon CR0 4YY

Scribe is committed to the sustainable use of natural resources and the use of paper products made responsibly from those resources.

9781 761381 94 2 (Australian edition)
978 1 917189 51 4 (UK edition)
978 1 761386 61 9 (ebook)

Catalogue records for this book are available from the National Library of Australia and the British Library.

scribepublications.com.au
scribepublications.co.uk
scribepublications.com

EU safety information: Easy Access System Europe, Mustamäe tee 50, 10621, Tallin, Estonia, gspr.requests@easproject.com.

BODY DOUBLE

I want to tell you. I'm going to.

THE IMAGE IS OF A DEPARTMENT STORE, A FAIRLY TIME-less image. Matte light, bluish. Beige marble, mirrors and chrome, two escalators that cross each other like a seam through the building. One going down, the other up. On the escalator going down is a woman. She's about thirty, perhaps a little younger, perhaps a little older; her outfit makes it hard to tell. She's wearing a camel-hair coat, a black turtleneck top, black pants, and leather boots. Her hair is dark and oiled, pushed behind her ears, where it ends just below the earlobes. Her eyes are dark, too. Her gaze distant. She would never admit to anyone how much time she spends on her looks. She keeps one hand on the escalator's handrail, which moves a little quicker than the escalator itself, and now and then she has to correct her grip. She puts her free hand in her pocket.

On the department store's downward escalator, with one hand on the handrail—which moves a little quicker than the escalator itself—Naomi puts her other, free hand in her coat pocket and knows that something isn't right. The surprise is dull. It hits her in the stomach and on the skin, the vertiginous feeling of discovering that something is off without knowing what. Like drinking from a glass of milk and expecting water. The still unspecified discovery makes her freeze, and when the escalator reaches the second floor of the department store—the menswear section—she checks both of her pockets. And now she realizes, with perfect clarity, that they've got the wrong things in them. Instead of her leather gloves, which were the reason she slipped her hand into her pocket, there's a heavy, metallic lipstick tube and a piece of paper. These are not her things: a fact she immediately understands. And when she feels the cool, slippery lining of the pocket against her bare hands she knows what caused that initial strong sense that something wasn't right. The lining of her own pockets isn't slippery. It's not supposed to feel like this lining, not this cool and silky. The lining of her own pockets is rough. Vertigo dissolves along with disbelief and yields to the pleasant feeling of things falling into place, receiving their logical explanation. Now she understands. She must have put on the wrong coat when she left the café. She put on a coat that looks just like hers, but which belongs to somebody else.

She takes off the coat and hangs it over her arm. To keep wearing it now, when she knows it doesn't belong to her, seems improper. She takes the escalator up again, to the third floor (furniture, textiles, the tea house, and the champagne bar), to the fourth floor (books, toys), and every floor is—still, though Christmas is over—decorated with artificial boughs and artificial holly, lanterns and red ribbon. Beige marble, mirrors, chrome. When she gets to the fifth floor, the one she just left, the floor with the department store's café and its view of the atrium and the enormous, illuminated tree towering down there, she sees a blond woman, facing away from her, putting first one arm and then the other into Naomi's coat, which is nearly identical to the one Naomi is currently holding over her arm.

She approaches her and puts a hand on her arm. The other woman turns around. Naomi notes that her lips are brown, painted. That's the first thing she sees. The second is her very pale eyes. She's got a pale face, sallow and sickly, with high cheekbones and a wide mouth.

I'm sorry, she says, it seems I took your coat by mistake, and now you've taken mine.

The woman looks at her, then at the coat hanging over her arm. She doesn't say anything.

She's attractive, Naomi thinks, and a little odd.

She laughs, nervously or, she hopes, disarmingly. I'm the one who should be apologizing, she continues, though the other woman hasn't made any move to apologize and though she herself has already said sorry. I started it. It was my mistake, entirely mine, I took it without thinking, I didn't even realize. I didn't realize until I was on my way down the escalator, but luckily I hadn't gotten any farther than that, no, it's lucky I didn't get any farther than that, if I'd made it all the way home we might never have been able to set it right.

The other woman stares at her, stares with her pale eyes. They seem unnaturally pale, those eyes, pale like the eyes of a blind person, with tiny pupils, and Naomi doesn't understand her expression, which seems devastated or frightened. Neither of these feelings are commensurate with the situation. She's still wearing Naomi's coat. She opens her brown lips, but no words come out. She checks inside the pockets as if looking for something, and only then does she seem to understand, only then does it seem like Naomi's message lands, and finally she takes off the coat, still without a word. Naomi holds out the coat she's kept on her arm, and the other woman holds out hers. They swap.

It's a common style, Naomi says and removes a blond hair from the collar of her coat.

It's a common style, the other woman agrees.

Her voice as she repeats the words is unsteady and brittle. She speaks as if she hadn't used her voice in ages. As if she's not used to speaking.

She keeps her coat in her arms while Naomi puts her coat on. Neither of them say anything else, and the silence between them makes Naomi feel as if the sounds around them are growing in strength: the silverware against the plates in the café, the din rising from the different floors of the department store, and the muted, nondescript music playing from the speakers.

She walks toward the escalator. The other woman remains in place. She stays there as Naomi steps on the escalator and begins the descent, and Naomi looks back one single time and meets the other woman's eyes, her pale, frightened eyes. Then Naomi turns, abruptly, and grabs the warm handrail, and she squeezes the leather gloves in the rough pocket, these leather gloves that are where they should be, and she looks at the hand that is holding on hard to the matte black handrail, watches as the hand moves a little too quickly, so that she now and then has to correct her grip, and though she would no longer be able to see the other woman if she turned she's got a strong sense that she is still standing next to the café table, looking in the direction Naomi went. I shouldn't have turned around, she thinks, shouldn't have looked as I left. I shouldn't have met her gaze.

When she gets off the escalator on the ground floor (beauty), she once again has a strong sense that the other woman is staring at her, with her unpleasantly pale eyes, and she's ill at ease at the thought of this stranger—Why was she staring like that? Why was she so quiet?—and ill at ease with a cold, slick feeling of guilt. She doesn't understand this feeling. She tries to catch it, but it escapes like a swift, slippery fish. I'm not guilty of anything, she thinks. I haven't done anything wrong. I didn't do anything wrong touching her arm. I didn't do anything wrong. I didn't do anything wrong when I turned around and looked at her. That's not illegal, is it? It's not so peculiar. Two strangers meet at a department store, that's completely normal, two strangers mix up each other's coats. That's completely normal. It's a common style, she thinks.

Sometime later they run into each other again. It's the same place. Naomi is at one of the café's round tables, stirring the contents of a small, pale-blue sachet of sweetener into her black coffee. A tiny white pill. She doesn't touch the chocolate that's included in the price of a coffee.

The other woman sees her first. She walks up to Naomi's table. This time she's got her coat over her arm. Her arrival makes Naomi look up from her coffee cup, look up from the dark swirl, and she drops the spoon. It clatters against the saucer.

Do you remember me? the other woman asks.

Her lips are painted the same brown shade as before, her eyes are just as pale, and her face is just as sallow, but her voice is no longer a whisper. It's strong and clear, and she smiles at Naomi, a tentative, unaccustomed smile.

Naomi returns the smile. Sure I remember you, she says.

Would you mind, the other woman asks, if I sat down?

Naomi sees no reason to say no, no normal reason. The other woman sits down at her table, facing her. She drapes her coat across her knees. She's dressed in black. Her style is simple. Looking at her, Naomi thinks that she is elegant. She's got no makeup on other than the brown lipstick. The color doesn't suit her, it makes her look even paler, more lifeless, but also, Naomi thinks, interesting.

I love your lipstick, Naomi says.

She tends to give a compliment when she's not sure what feeling she inspires in someone.

I'm Naomi, she continues. How about you, what's your name?

Before the other woman can answer, a waiter dressed

in black and white comes to take her order. She asks for an espresso and a bottle of sparkling water. The waiter asks if she would like a glass with ice. The other woman asks for two glasses with ice and a big bottle. She turns to Naomi.

Do you want water?

Yes, sure. Why not?

Two glasses with ice, the waiter repeats, a big bottle, and he leaves.

The woman looks after him. She seems lost in thought. Eventually she turns back to Naomi. She says nothing, and Naomi repeats her question.

What's your name?

The woman looks at her for so long and with such a vacant expression that Naomi again feels as if she's committed a mistake, and she opens her mouth to apologize even as an irked, lonely feeling rises in her. That's an absolutely normal question. She's done nothing wrong. But before Naomi can say anything, the other woman answers, spitting it out as if she's just thought of the answer to a riddle:

Laura.

That's all she says, and Naomi smiles mildly, for Laura's sake or her own. She blows on her coffee. She wants to look somewhere else. She doesn't know what they're meant to talk about. She doesn't know what Laura wants from her. Laura is a stranger who's sat down at Naomi's table. She's got an odd way about her. Naomi has never experienced anyone acting this way before. Laura's interest in her is confusing, but also flattering.

The waiter returns with Laura's espresso, the two

glasses with ice in them, and a big glass bottle of sparkling water. There's steam when he opens the bottle cap and a hissing, crackling sound as the water hits the ice. The ice cubes break. The waiter sets the bottle on the table and leaves.

There's so little left in the bottle, Naomi notes, that it won't be enough for two additional full glasses. Two small glasses, however, or one full and one with very little in it. It's not a big deal. She wouldn't have given it a thought if she were sharing the bottle with someone she knew. But the person she's sharing the bottle with is a stranger, as of yet a stranger, and she doesn't know how they will collaborate. No, she knows nothing about the person facing her. She knows nothing about why she's offered her water.

Laura is holding the ear of her small white cup, holds the cup in the air, but doesn't drink from it. She looks Naomi in the eye.

You scared me last time, she says.

I did? Naomi says.

I'm sure you noticed, Laura says, but I can't imagine you understood why. I think you thought I was a bit odd.

Naomi smiles. She drinks from her water. There's a smarting feeling when the ice hits her teeth. And she makes a decision. Normally she would say that she hadn't noticed anything at all, that Laura didn't seem odd at all, because that's what she imagines to be the right answer, but this time she's going to be honest. It costs her nothing to be honest. They might never meet again. Laura, she thinks, in a dizzying realization, doesn't need to like her. She doesn't need to make Laura like her.

You're right, she says. I didn't understand why you were so upset. That's what I thought, at any rate: that you were upset. I went home with a terrible feeling of having made a mistake.

I'm sorry, Laura says.

It's fine, Naomi says. I often feel that way.

Laura laughs. Like you've made a mistake?

Yes. Is that so strange?

I don't know.

Yes. No—yes, it's absolutely true that I often feel that way.

What makes you feel that way?

All kinds of things. I don't know. Being late. Or being too early. Getting lost. Knowing what I want to tell someone but not being able to say it out loud. Or saying the wrong thing. I don't know. All kinds of things make me feel as if I've made a mistake.

That doesn't sound like an easy life, Laura says.

Naomi laughs. She drinks from her water. I'm kind of joking with you, she says, and Laura adds nothing. They're silent for a moment.

Why did I scare you? Naomi eventually asks.

Laura casts her eyes down. With a vacant expression she begins to push down the cuticle of her pointer finger with her thumb. She's got long fingers and short nails, and her knuckles are a little dry.

Then she looks at Naomi again.

It had been a long time since I'd spoken to anyone, she says. And this is something I haven't been able to talk to anyone about. I haven't had anyone I could talk to.

She holds her coffee cup, her small white espresso cup, with both hands. She pauses for a beat.

Lately I've had the sense that I've disappeared, she says.

Naomi doesn't know how to respond. She blows on her coffee and drinks. The artificial sweetener is potent.

I don't want you to think that I'm crazy, Laura says.

I don't know you well enough to not think that you're crazy, Naomi says. It's an attempt to lighten the mood. But Laura doesn't laugh; Laura is completely serious. This makes Naomi serious, too, and she puts down her coffee cup.

What do you mean? she asks. What do you mean you've disappeared?

It's hard to explain, Laura says.

Try, Naomi says.

Laura hesitates.

It feels, she says, tentatively, as if I've lost myself.

She lowers her gaze and starts to push down her cuticle again. Naomi waits for the continuation. She looks at Laura's lowered gaze, at her mouth. She waits for Laura to find the words, but Laura is silent, wholly focused on the cuticle of her pointer finger, the movement of the thumbnail.

I think I understand what you mean, Naomi says, finally. I was left once.

Laura stops fidgeting and looks at her.

Left? she asks.

Yes, says Naomi. By someone I was living with. It was out of the blue, from one day to the next. After that I, too, had a sense of having disappeared. Or of having lost myself.

Laura looks intently at her.

That's exactly what happened to me, she says. Yes. That's what happened. I was left.

She drinks from her little white cup, a small sip, and Naomi looks at her chapped hands. She's gripping the cup's ear hard, but her hand is shaking. The cup clatters against the saucer when she puts it down.

And since then I've had such an odd feeling, Laura continues. It's as if I had a doppelgänger.

A doppelgänger? Naomi says.

A doppelgänger, Laura says. Yes. I've had this sense that there are two of me. I've found myself in places where I've been before but which I no longer know. I recognize my surroundings as if from a dream. I've got this sense that my life—the life that used to be mine—is continuing somewhere though I can't participate in it anymore. Yes. I've had this sense that my life has moved on without me. That's the best way I can explain it.

I understand exactly what you mean, Naomi says.

You do? Laura says.

Yes, says Naomi, I understand exactly. When I was left it was as if my life went on without me. I used to be able to see the future with perfect clarity and suddenly it was all gone, even though it had never existed. It was like having phantom pain.

Phantom pain, Laura repeats.

I felt as if I'd been split in half, Naomi continues, and she's surprised by the words that gush from her now, surprised by this memory she's not touched in many years but which she suddenly, face to face with this unfamiliar woman, wants to share.

It still feels that way, she says, as if I've been split in half. Or as if I was pushed to a fork in the road. As if a part of me, a part I can no longer reach, still lives the life I lived back then, still lives in that future I imagined for myself, walking down that path I was walking back then, while I—I mean this version of me...

She falls silent.

I had to create a new life for myself, she says. I had to become someone else.

Yes, Laura says. Exactly. Exactly.

With shaking hands, she brings the little white coffee cup back to her lips.

When I saw you, she says, when you touched me and made me turn around.

Yes, Naomi says.

It made me think of a scene in a movie, Laura says. Or a memory. It was as if I knew what would happen from the very beginning. As if everything had already happened. In that moment, when I turned around and looked you in the eye, in that moment I was seized by this terrible fear. It overwhelmed me, completely. I thought, in that moment, that it was you who'd become my new life.

Me? says Naomi.

Yes, Laura says. You. That's what I thought.

She looks at Naomi, looks at her with the same expression as that first time, the same intensely pale and fearful, demanding, but also strangely frank gaze, and Naomi feels that she should get up from her chair, that she should leave. She has the sense that her life, if she stays, is going to change.

But the moment is over before she can act, and Laura smiles.

That's what I thought, she says again. But then I understood. It was just—it was just because I'd taken your coat that you made me turn around.

Naomi smiles. Then she laughs, relieved and confused.

I'm not sure I understand, she says.

Me neither, Laura says. I didn't really understand it myself afterward, after that feeling had faded. After I'd watched you ride down the escalator again.

I saw you watching me, Naomi says. I had this feeling that you were standing there, looking, for a long while.

I did, Laura says. It's true.

Laura pours Naomi some more water. She's not yet touched her own.

You come here a lot, Laura says.

Naomi can't tell from her tone of voice if it's a statement or a question. But it is true that she often comes to the department store café.

Yes, Naomi says. I come here a lot.

I have seen you, Laura says. Since the first time we met, since you took my coat. Several times. You're alone.

Once again Naomi can't quite tell if what Laura is saying is a question or not. And it's true that she often comes to the department store café alone. That she always comes alone. Laura is right.

I usually come here alone, she confirms. I like to come here and relax for a moment. Sometimes I'll come here for a little while after work instead of going straight home. I like being here. Among other people who are in motion. It makes me feel calm.

She drinks from her water and now Laura, too, drinks, for the first time during their conversation, from her water.

Have you seen me? Laura asks.

No, Naomi says. Never before you took my coat, and not after, either.

Laura fills up Naomi's glass again.

I agree, it is relaxing here, she says. I like coming here, too. Alone.

I used to work here when I was younger, Naomi says.

Really? Laura asks.

Yes, Naomi says. When I was eighteen. When I'd just moved to the city. On the ground floor, in the beauty department.

The beauty department, Laura repeats. And still you come back.

Yes, Naomi says.

One might think, Laura says, that you'd be sick of the place. After working here.

Yes, Naomi says, that's what I thought would happen when I worked here. That I'd never want to come back. I thought I'd be sick of it all, I thought the scent of perfume would make me feel nauseous, but that never happened. I've always liked being here. It didn't take away any of the glamour, working at the perfume counter. No, I still think there's something glamorous about this place. Truly. Even though I used to work here. I still feel that there's a kind of magic to it. Even though everything looks so different when you're on the other side. It is like being onstage compared to being in the audience.

Naomi stops. She's surprised by her own enthusiasm for the subject. She's never thought much about what it means that she used to work in the department store a long time ago and that she now likes to visit as a customer.

Laura smiles at her. Are you an actress? she asks, and Naomi says, No, why? The stage, Laura says. And the audience.

Oh, that, Naomi says. It was just a comparison. I've never been onstage, never wanted to. No, I've only ever been in the audience. Right where we are now, you might say.

So we're surrounded by actors, then, Laura says and looks toward the waiter in black and white who is clearing a table with swift, graceful movements.

Most of the time I feel like an extra, Naomi says, but it doesn't bother me.

An extra? Laura repeats.

Yes, Naomi says, someone with no lines, someone who's just there to make the world feel populated.

Someone who's there to make the world feel populated, Laura repeats. She pushes her blond hair behind her ears. It reaches her shoulders.

Do you dye your hair? asks Naomi.

Laura laughs. What an odd question.

I'm sorry, I was just so curious. It's an unusual color. A beautiful color.

Thank you, that's kind, Laura says. It's my natural

color. It grows like this, straight out of my head. How about you? Do you dye your hair?

No, Naomi says. No, that's something I've never done. Never dared to do it. I don't know why, it might sound silly, but I can't bear the thought of not recognizing my own reflection.

You think it would have that effect, Laura says, dyeing your hair? Something that small? That it would cause you to not recognize yourself?

Naomi shakes her head. I know. It sounds silly. It's some kind of superstition. Also I'm worried it would ruin my hair.

Yes, Laura says, dyeing the hair damages it, I've heard that, too, it's true. Bleaching it, especially. And your hair, it could hardly be much darker.

No, Naomi agrees.

So if you were to dye it, Laura says, you'd have to bleach it.

Yes, Naomi says.

They fall silent.

Exactly, Naomi says just to say something, and Laura doesn't reply, says nothing at all.

This idea that you wouldn't recognize yourself, she says, finally. It's like at the theater.

What is? Naomi asks.

This idea that it would be that easy to take on a new identity, Laura says. Simply by changing hair color. Someone pulls on a wig or a hat, and suddenly not even their own parents recognize them, not even their closest friends...

Naomi laughs. You're right. Yes. It probably doesn't work like that in real life. No, not in real life. For better or for worse.

Do you go to the theater a lot? Laura asks.

Sometimes, Naomi says. It happens. Not that often. I prefer the movies. I love films.

She takes another sip from her cup, drinks of the sweet, bitter coffee, which has cooled by now and is almost too cold to drink. She drinks to slow down. She thinks: I talk too much.

But Laura smiles when she looks at her, her pale eyes shining with interest. What kinds of movies? she asks. What kinds of movies do you love?

Ah, Naomi says, all kinds of things. Romantic movies...movies about, you know, a widow who falls in love with her gardener. I love movies like that. Yes: a couple saying goodbye at a train station ... yes ... those kinds of movies I love. Romantic movies, yes. But I watch all kinds of things. Thrillers...ghost stories...do you know what I love most of all?

Laura shakes her head. She drinks from her espresso. No. Tell me.

I love movies about paranoid women, Naomi says with a laugh. Women who live alone. Women who are stalked. Women who are driven mad. And women who are murdered. Is that terrible?

Not to me, Laura says. A lot of people find violence entertaining. Is that what you like about them, the violence?

No, Naomi says. No, those scenes are almost always too drawn out. I find them boring.

I agree with you, Laura says.

It's not the murder itself that interests me. No, those movies would probably be better without the murder at the end. But a lonely woman listening for a strange sound ... a woman who's being stalked, or gripped by paranoia ... I don't know ... I don't know how to explain it. For some reason that's the best thing I know. Sometimes I actually feel like one of those women myself. You know, the imagination can run wild at night.

Yes, Laura says. I know what you mean.

They fall silent.

Do you live alone? Laura asks.

Yes, Naomi says, and Laura says nothing more.

Naomi smiles and looks down. I don't know why I'm telling you all this, she says. Well, I asked, Laura says. True. Yes. You did ask.

Naomi drinks from her water and when she puts it down on the table Laura fills it again, for the last time. The bottle is empty. The waiter in black and white removes the bottle and the empty coffee cups, leaving the water glasses. Laura pays with coins. The waiter leaves. They sit in silence for a brief moment before Laura leans forward. Her hands are folded. She holds them as if they were hiding something.

It was nice to meet you, Naomi, she says. Thanks for letting me sit at your table. I wanted to explain myself. I wanted to explain why you scared me. It wasn't your fault.

She leans back in the chair again.

These past few weeks, she says, there have been several times when I almost walked up to you. I almost walked up and asked if I could sit down, but I could never do it. Every time there was something stopping me. It wasn't fear. No, not at that point. It was about something else. I could stand there and watch you for a long while but I didn't dare to approach. Isn't that funny? I guess you made me shy. I don't know why.

Her voice is relaxed. The revelation smashes into Naomi like a dull sledgehammer.

Laura puts on her coat, Naomi puts on hers, and they ride the escalator down in silence. Naomi first and then Laura, behind her. Laura watches Naomi's neck. She watches the shiny, dark hair, the white shirt collar that peeks out of the coat's collar, the pink earlobes. The hand that rests on the handrail, which moves a little faster than the escalator itself, the hand with long fingers and short, well-manicured nails. They ride together to the street level, the beauty department, and Laura glances at the young women behind the perfume counter. Together they walk toward the big, heavy glass doors. Laura pushes them open and lets Naomi walk out first. Then she follows her onto the street. She takes a deep breath, pulling the dry, frigid air into her lungs.

It smells like fire, she says and looks at Naomi. Yes, Naomi says. You're right, when the temperature drops the city starts to smell like fire.

She looks into Laura's pale eyes. The sharp winter light makes her pupils very small.

Will I see you again? she says.

Yes, Laura says. You will.

Naomi squeezes the leather gloves in her pocket with one hand, and offers the other, free hand to Laura, who takes it in her own. She presses it. Her hand is rough and cold.

Now you're not a stranger anymore, Naomi says. Now I know your name.

WHEN THE TEMPERATURE DROPS THE CITY STARTS TO smell like fire. I take the metro before the sun is up, I stamp my ticket, it's sucked into the machine and spat out again, BANG. I stand in the clattering train, I listen to the chiming of the doors. I hold on to a leather strap. I hold on to keep my balance. The train is full of people. The train is crowded. Every seat is taken and a hand hangs from every strap. I rest my eyes. I close them for a while and open them again. I look at my own reflection in the train's scratched windows, I look at the other passengers, I look at them closing their eyes, look at them looking out the window, look at them looking at their own reflection, look at them reading the free newspaper. The paper is called CITY. The paper is about living in a city. It tells us everything about the events of the day and the night, it tells us what to do and where to go: to Submondo, to Rigardi. I read over the shoulder of the man next to me until he folds the paper and slides it under his arm.

The train barrels through the darkness. It rises out of the tunnels and stops at the station where I get off, an aboveground station. It's an old station, almost a hundred years old, a wrought iron structure above the big, clamorous street below.

I exit the train and step into the dark morning. I walk down the stairs and onto the street. It smells like fire.

I walk to the ghostwriter's office. It's not far. The

streetlamps are still lit, illuminating the pavement for me as I pass the laundromat, where the machines are spinning and frothing in the sharp overhead light, as I pass the bakery, where the flour billows. The chilly air smells of warm bread and laundry detergent. I spot the glow from the ghostwriter's basement window even before I arrive at his office. A yellow rectangle on the sidewalk. I walk down the stairs, push open the heavy door to the basement, and enter the office, just like I do every week. Now I'm on the other side. Now I'm inside the bright, yellow room. Outside the little windowpane, out on the sidewalk, it's pitch-black.

I work for the ghostwriter. That's what I do. That's who I am.

Every week I come here. Once early in the week, once at the end of the week. It's always the same thing, always the same way. I could walk the route in my sleep, or with my eyes closed. No problem. I'm so used to my routine that it barely feels as if it's me going through the motions: stamping the ticket, holding on to the strap to keep my balance on the train, pushing the basement door open. It is my hand, but it could have belonged to a stranger. I see everything. I think nothing.

The ghostwriter gives me this week's tapes. We drink a little cup of coffee together. His desk is littered with detritus. Sheets of paper. Ballpoint pens. The ghostwriter likes to take notes by hand, and his notes are scattered all over. The ghostwriter smokes a cigarette and flicks the ash into a black glass ashtray. There's a weeping fig in his office that doesn't get enough sunlight. Its leaves are yellow and sparse. He compliments my coat.

I like your coat, he says.
My coat is almost the same as his. A long trench coat.
Thanks, I say.
He points out the coincidence.
It's almost the same as mine, he says.
It's a common style.

The ghostwriter and I always chat for a bit when I stop by his office. Not about anything important. He asks if I've had a nice weekend. I ask if he's had a nice weekend. He often praises the past week's transcriptions. I'm a good listener. I'm quick and efficient. Without me he wouldn't be able to do his work. Without our collaboration he wouldn't be as good of a ghostwriter.

Soon enough it's time for me to leave the ghostwriter's office. I thank him for the coffee. Then I head home. I head home with this week's tapes, and I get to work.

I listen to the recordings. I transcribe. That's what I do. For hours I listen, every week. I listen, diligently, and I write down exactly what I hear.

If you buy the ghostwriter's services you'll receive a cassette player and ten tapes with ninety minutes of recording time each. It's not the most modern way to record sound. But it's simple. The tapes are cheap. The ghostwriter likes them.

I like them, too.

I like the image of the tape being rolled up.

When you buy the ghostwriter's services you receive, in addition to the cassette player and the ten tapes with ninety minutes of recording time each, an instruction manual. This manual has a hard cover made of cardboard. The ghostwriter binds his instruction manuals himself. They're beautiful, like little works of art. His customers feel reassured to receive such a beautiful instruction manual; it makes the ghostwriter's services appear serious. It speaks to high quality. If the finished product is even half as beautiful as the instruction manual, one might think, then the ghostwriter's services are well worth the cost.

The ghostwriter has written the instruction book to explain how the individual purchasing his services should proceed in sharing the story of her life.

Make yourself at ease, the instruction manual says. It's a good idea to get comfortable in a chair, perhaps an armchair or a couch. You might want to pour yourself a glass of wine, if that helps you to start talking. If it helps you get at the truth. You might want to record yourself in the evening to eliminate any risk of interruption. Feel free to stay up all night telling your story if you find that the words are coming to you. But of course, if the morning or the middle of the day is when you're least likely to be interrupted, you can record then. You choose. Do what suits you best. Your needs are central. This is your own story. It's not a problem if you doze off during recording. As long as you feel calm, safe, and comfortable. Take your time, the instruction manual says.

The ghostwriter's task is not to judge anyone. That's his most important rule. He repeats it often, he reminds me of it. It is not my task to judge anyone, either. We must make the clients feel that they're in safe hands. He works hard to make them feel this way. Some of them must be convinced. Not everyone, he says, has had a good experience when they've told the story of their lives. No. They might have reason to hesitate. Some might have been exploited over things they've shared. They might not have been believed. They might have been mistreated. They might have been abandoned because of something they said. It is important for the ghostwriter to win their trust. It is important to him—he tells me this often—that the two of us can trust each other, too.

He writes in his instruction manual: There's no need to embellish or hide anything. Nothing can shock me anymore. Trust me. Tell the story of your life as truthfully as possible. Without judgment. Without holding back. Without irony. Are there things you are ashamed of? Are there things you regret? Are there things you've never forgiven yourself for? Do you have weaknesses? Have you done terrible things? Things that would ruin your life if somebody knew? I want to know it all. I will never be upset with you. I want you to tell me everything. It is important for our work.

The ghostwriter wants as much material as possible. It's never a problem to share too much, or to tell the same story twice. On the contrary, he encourages it. Having multiple angles is helpful. It's useful. A much more difficult problem is when somebody is unable to speak at all. Some of the ghostwriter's clients let the recording roll without being able to produce even a single word. They're not prepared for how difficult it is.

Tell your story as straightforwardly as you can, the instruction manual says. I invite you to use your senses. Do you remember what things used to smell like? What they tasted like? Do you remember their sounds? Try to remember. Try to remember the details. You may speak in lists, for instance: all the games you would play as a child, all the movies you watched in the theater, all the pets, all your friends, and so on. Everything that comes to mind. The things that seem obvious to you, or even insignificant, are what give the story its color and thrust. I am interested in everything that's ever happened to you. Everything you've ever thought. Everything you've felt. You don't need to be concerned with a coherent narrative. You don't need to be concerned with a beautiful narrative. The structure, the metaphors, and the beauty of the prose—I'll take care of all of that later. That is my job.

Few of the ghostwriter's clients are able to tell their story without value judgments, without guarding themselves, without irony, despite his clear instructions. I remember a woman who described the first time she met her husband: I guess he wasn't a great beauty, but then again nobody has accused me of being one, either...

Another liked to use literary turns of phrase: When he kissed me it was as if a thousand birds took off from a tree...

Despite the ghostwriter's instructions to his clients to share things they are ashamed of, things they regret, I often have the sense that they are hiding something from him—or, rather, from themselves. I believe that they're sharing smaller things they are ashamed of or regret so they won't have to talk about the big things they are ashamed of or regret. Their hesitation and their silences reveal a lot to me and the ghostwriter. Sometimes you can tell from their tone of voice that they've experienced things far worse than what they're telling us. Sometimes they don't realize it themselves.

The ghostwriter is expensive. It's not exactly a service for everyone. His clients are women who already have it all, who don't know what else to do with their money.

Everyone who buys the ghostwriter's services is a woman. He doesn't know why, though he has his theories. He awakens the mother in them. He looks so young. Deceptively young. He looks boyish though he must be comfortably middle-aged. What is it about him that makes him look so boyish? Is it his rosy, beardless cheeks? Is it his eyes? Is it his thick hair? Is it his slender build, his small hands, narrow shoulders?

Whatever the case may be, his boyishness inspires their tenderness. That he knows. And he shows them care. He takes care of them. He takes care of them as if he were their son.

The women who buy the ghostwriter's services are eager to tell someone about their lives. They are eager to feel that they've lived. They want someone to listen to them, they want there to be proof that they existed once they're gone, they want there to be something that survives them, something that will never die.

The first time I heard a woman describe a rape, I called the ghostwriter. What do we do with this? I asked him. Call the police? No, he told me. I don't think there's any point. It's hard to prove.

The first time I heard a woman describe a murder, I called the ghostwriter again. What do we do with this? I asked him. Call the police?

He hesitated for a long time. So long I thought the call had dropped. I asked if he was still there. Yes, he replied.

Then he hesitated for another moment.

No, he eventually replied.

Both of us were silent at our end of the line but neither hung up.

My work is not to judge anyone, he said. Nor is it yours.

Over time the ghostwriter has built up a reputation. He's always booked.

That means I'm also booked.

It is common for the ghostwriter's clients to buy far more tapes than the ten included in the base price. That adds another fee. Not only to cover the cost of the tape, but also my work transcribing the recordings, and the ghostwriter's work processing the material. Many of them have a lot to say. Many of them have lived long lives.

I grow attached to the women. I spend weeks with their recordings. They're there every morning when I turn on my computer. I sit by my kitchen window and listen to their stories. I get to know them. I keep the tapes, not to listen again but because I worry they might get into the wrong hands if I got rid of them, if I lost track of them. Nobody can know what's on these recordings. Nobody but the ghostwriter and me.

I often remember details from the women's lives after I've transcribed their stories, but ultimately they all blend together in my memory. A lot of the women have similar experiences. It's inevitable to mix up the stories when you hear this many people describe their lives. But while working I'm diligent. I listen, and I listen again.

I type out what they say. Exactly what they say. Every word, even when the words don't make full sentences. I write out their silences and pauses.

Many of the women need to take a moment before they find the words. They need to sit there, alone, with the tape rolling.

When that happens we wait together.

I listen to a woman who is trying to find the words.

My childhood... she says.

A long silence follows.

I type: My childhood...

Her silence lasts for several minutes. I write: Silence.

Then she says, anew: My childhood... my childhood... was happy... nothing remarkable...

We wait together. I listen to the whirring of the tape and look at the marker that blinks, impatient, on the screen. But I'm in no rush.

I've never thought much about my childhood, she says. And now it strikes me... that I don't know...

The tape rolls, crackles. I listen. I type.

...whether it was happy... Maybe it doesn't matter. I always thought... that a childhood... I wish I had something to tell you. But I simply, I simply don't remember anything...

She falls silent. I type.

Details, she says, as if to herself.

Then she's silent for a long while.

Oh, darnit, she says. No... This is no good... this is just no good... no... I don't have what it takes to do it... I don't have what it takes...

She begins to cry. But she doesn't stop the recording.

I listen as she weeps and I wait with her. I write that she's crying. It could be helpful for the ghostwriter to know.

A lot of them feel it's hard to start talking. But almost all of them eventually find a way to tell their story. Almost everyone can find something to remember.

I've received my own instructions from the ghostwriter. I am to listen carefully. I am to write down everything. Write down exactly what I hear. Type out the silences and the pauses. Type out if they cry, laugh, scoff, or contort their voice. Type out the exact sequence of words, even when it seems incoherent. Type out every single word. I am to be diligent about their choice of words. I am to be diligent about their silence. It can tell something important. It can reveal something valuable. It can reveal what is painful in the women's lives, or what has brought them joy.

It is the ghostwriter who finds the structure and organizing conflict of every life. He writes a story. He finds the captivating introductory scene. He finds the right language. He finds the coincidences. He finds the details that make everything seem coherent and imbued with a deeper meaning. He writes his books as if the women were already dead. This grants the story a certain splendor. The ghostwriter's books are poignant and melancholy. They inspire the reader to contemplate life's beauty and fragility. His clients are pleased to be remembered in such a way. The women feel pleased to remember themselves this way even as they're still alive.

Once the ghostwriter has finished a woman's story, he binds it into a book. He does it all himself. He is very skilled. It's good craftsmanship. The women receive the book in the mail, wrapped in tissue paper. The books always look the same. They all have red covers. They all have the same title: Story of a Life.

I've often considered the possibility that the women are lying. That they might be willfully straying from the ghostwriter's instructions to tell the truth. Not lying in the sense of keeping secrets or hiding one truth with another—but lying as in fully making things up, telling stories that have not happened to them at all, things that have happened to someone else or that they've read in a book or in the paper, things they've seen in a movie, things they've thought up or fantasized about. Things they wish would have happened, or things they're instead relieved didn't happen. Dramatic things. Violent things.

It is impossible for me to know what is true and what isn't. I know nothing about the women other than what they tell. They might very well be telling entirely fake versions of their lives, a story made up of lies from beginning to end. But that doesn't matter for my work. I only write down what I hear.

That is all I can do.

At the end of the week I take the metro: BANG. It's morning but it looks like night. I've got my pages in a folder that I'm pressing to my chest. I give the ghostwriter my pages. He thanks me. We've got a good working relationship. I leave the office and the pavement sparkles, the air smells like fire, it smells of warm bread and detergent as I walk past the bakery, where the flour billows, and the laundromat, where the machines are spinning, and when I come up the stairs to the platform a flash goes off inside the photo booth and the receiver in the doorless phone booth adjacent to it is bouncing on its cord. I walk up and return it to the hook. A woman bumps into me when I turn around, she's walking at full speed, she shoves my shoulder so hard I almost lose my balance. I don't see her face, I only feel her body. I don't have time to look before she disappears in the direction of the trains. The station is crowded. Lots of people in a hurry.

While I'm waiting for my train I buy a coffee and a croissant with apricot filling at the station kiosk. The croissant is soft. I take a paper sachet of sugar and tear it open with my teeth. I stir the white sugar into my coffee with a thin wooden stick. The coffee is hot and sweet. The croissant is sweet. I look at the magazines in the kiosk. I'd like to buy a lipstick. A brown lipstick. I buy a magazine and I'm just able to pay and get my change in coins before the train barrels into the station.

I hold on to a leather strap, I keep my balance, I look at the other passengers, they're reading books, they're reading CITY, they're sitting and standing in the crowded train and I've got the magazine under my arm, pressing it hard against my body. The glossy cover is slippery. I've burned my tongue on the hot, sweet coffee. The apricot filling covers my teeth with a film. The train roars underground, clattering through the tunnels, the white lights flicker as we pass.

I'm free now. I have money from the ghostwriter. I'm free to do whatever I want. By the time I exit the train and walk up the stairs and onto the street, the sun is up. The day has begun.

I roll up the magazine and hold it in my hand, and with my other hand, my free hand, I check my pocket. I check for my sheet of paper.

I unlock the narrow door to my building and I cross the yard, the yard with the tall tree and the trash cans, and I enter through the next door and walk up the stairs and the whole time I keep my hand on the paper in my pocket. I'm checking to make sure it's there as I walk upstairs—the stairwell is cold today, my stairwell where the windows have frost on them today. The steps, shiny from wear, creak beneath my feet. I quickly climb all five sets of stairs and pause, for just a moment, on the landing in front of my door. I can hear my phone ring in there. One ring. I unlock the door and turn on the lamp in the hall. I drop my keys in the stoneware bowl on the table by the door and then I empty the coins from my pocket; they land in the bowl with a clatter. I listen for another ring but it never comes. I didn't get to it in time. I put down the magazine, hang up my coat, and take my shoes off. I check my answering machine. Nobody has left any messages. They always call back if it's important.

I take the piece of paper from my coat pocket, the sheet I've folded four times. It's a transcription I haven't given to the ghostwriter. I've never done this before. I've never kept anything from the ghostwriter. I've never kept any secrets from him. I know how important it is to him that we can trust each other. I know it's wrong of me to keep the sheet. Everything I type I give him. Every word. I write down everything I hear, and I give him the words.

But this is different. I've never heard anything like it before. It's not like a rape or a murder. It's not something I can ask the ghostwriter to help me with. I don't think he can help me this time.

Transcription work requires great focus. You can't just sit there and doze off. You have to listen carefully to every word. You have to rewind and listen again, several times. You have to listen to the silence and be ready to start typing at any moment. I am receptive to every indication that the women might be about to start talking. Every change in their silence, their breathing. When you least expect it they'll inhale. When you least expect it they begin to tell their story.

I'm so lonely! Sometimes it feels . . . it feels as if I can't breathe! I wake up in the morning and everything is torturous! Yes, everything is absolutely, completely torturous! Torturous! I don't know what to do . . . it's torture to get dressed. Torture to . . . everything is torture! Splashing my face with cold water in the morning. I loathe it! I loathe putting my feet on the cold floor when I wake up! I should have gotten carpet. I really should have gotten carpet. But here we are. Oh, how I hate it. I hate my cold floors. And going outside for fresh air. But I hate staying inside, too. Sometimes I'll stay in my warm bed—I just can't bear to leave it, to put my feet on the floor . . . but it always leaves me terribly downcast. Yes. It makes me so very downcast. And it makes me feel so lonely. It's unbearable. Just impossible. All I do, I think, I do in order to forget . . . I don't know quite what . . . and I want, listen, I'll tell you this, I want you to write this! Write that I'm lonely! I want everyone to know. I want everyone to know that if I were to die tomorrow, then I would die unhappy!

I stood there and watched his train as it left the station, and I pictured him getting off at his stop ... walking home, unlocking his door ... right ... with his key ... and his wife—yes—I'm sure she met him in the foyer when he arrived—or perhaps upstairs? And I wondered if he would tell her that he'd met such a nice woman—"We went for lunch and saw a movie"—and suddenly I realized he never would! I knew it, with every fiber in my body! He would not say a word! And in that moment, that's when I felt it: I was flooded with the first, terrible feeling of danger!

I was bright in school, one of the best in our class. I sat in the front row, always raised my hand, I always knew the answer. Many of the other students were envious because I knew so much. They couldn't understand where I had learned it all. How I was able to remember everything—spelling, years ... The thing is, I have a photographic memory. I am able to memorize a phone number just by looking at it. I have never needed a calendar or an address book. I remember everything. Just by looking once ... at least I think I could still do it. It's been a long time now ... a long time since I had to remember anything new ... but I think I could still do it. It's something I've been able to do all my life. I never forget a face or a name. It's still there, all of it, every memory ... every face ... I have an enormous archive of faces inside me ... and names ... yes, lots of people were envious of me. Jealousy and envy have always been my least favorite sentiments. And resentment. We'll never get anywhere if we resent each other for our accomplishments. I've always believed that. Yes. Women in particular like to resent each other for this or that. Yes. We'll never get anywhere if we continue like this, that's always been a firm conviction of mine. I've always preferred the company of men...they're more straightforward. They've always appreciated my intelligence...

I was so young when my father passed away that I've never had any memories of him. I had two older brothers, both dead by now. I never asked them about our father. They remembered him. But it was...it was simply not discussed...My mother...she was vain. She was very attractive as a young woman. I've seen photographs. Yes, she was attractive...and dressed well, she did...old photographs...but for as long as I knew her she wouldn't let anyone photograph her. For as long as I knew her, my whole life with her, she was ugly. From the inside and out. Details...how can I put this... she had angry little eyes, bad breath...

IT HAD BEEN DARK OUTSIDE FOR A LONG TIME ALREADY when I put the week's final tape in my cassette player.

I was at my kitchen table. I always work at the kitchen table. I looked out the window and saw, across the yard, the windows of the neighboring buildings. Yellow squares. I saw my neighbors like shadows in there. It's too far for me to see them properly, and there is a tree in the yard, whose branches block the view. I rested my eyes and listened carefully as the recording started. I listened to the tape's spinning silence. No voice had yet begun to speak. I waited for the voice.

We waited together.

I waited for several minutes, listening for the rhythm of breath, but I heard nothing. Not a sound, nothing other than the sound of the tape. I waited with my hands prone and still at the keyboard. I looked at the windows and the shadows. I was careful not to let my mind wander. It took effort. It was late. My hands were tired from typing all week, my head was tired from listening all week. But soon I'd be done, again, I would be done like I am every week, ready to drop my pages off with the ghostwriter and receive my money. I was waiting for the voice. I was waiting for the familiar, dramatic inhale.

But it never came.

The voice came, instead, as if out of nowhere. Without preamble. It was as if somebody had cut the inhalation. The voice began to talk entirely without prelude, all naked. It was brittle, like a whisper, and it said: I have seen you. Have you seen me?

The recording stopped.

I typed: I have seen you. Have you seen me?

I rewound the tape and listened again. At first I didn't hear anything. I listened for the inhalation, more attentively this time, even more attentively than the first time, but I didn't hear anything. Only the whisper, as if from nowhere. I have seen you. Have you seen me?

Then nothing.

I rewound the tape, took it out of the machine, and inspected it. I wondered if there was something wrong with it. If it was broken. But it didn't look like the tape was broken. It didn't look like there was anything wrong with it.

I listened to it for a third time, this time with my hands resting in my lap and without being ready to type anything. I looked at the words in front of me, the words that matched the whisper on the tape. I looked at the blinking marker on the screen. I took the tape out again and put it down. I got up from my chair. I read the words on the screen, I read them several times. I printed the transcription, watching the printer as it spat out the paper. I watched the sentences being printed upside down, from the top to the bottom.

I have seen you. Have you seen me?

I placed the sheet of paper in the stack with my other pages, the pages I'd already printed, the pages I was going to deliver to the ghostwriter like I always did, pages full of words and life. On top of that stack I put my sheet of paper, the nearly empty sheet of paper, with the two sentences up top.

Then I turned off my computer and went outside for a walk. I walked along the canal in the darkness. I walked to the supermarket and bought a big bottle of sparkling water and a rotisserie chicken. At the register I had an impulse and went back to the fruit section, where I got a box of grapes. Green. I paid for my groceries. I held the bag under my arm as I unlocked the narrow door to my building, as I crossed the yard, entered through the next door, and walked up the stairs. With my free hand I held on to the banister, shiny from wear, and I walked up the stairs, the five sets of stairs, moving slowly. I drank a glass of sparkling water. I ate half the chicken. I rinsed the grapes, but then I changed my mind. I didn't want them anymore. I put them in a bowl and placed the bowl in the fridge. I brushed my teeth, washed my face, and brushed my hair in front of the bathroom mirror. Then I went to bed, and I lay in the dark and listened to the silence in my apartment and I thought: I am alone.

My mind casts back to everything I did after hearing the voice: the walk, the supermarket, the chicken and the grapes, my face in the mirror as I brushed my teeth and brushed my hair. My memory of the hours before I heard the recording is nowhere near as detailed. I don't know exactly what I was doing. I know more or less. I worked. I looked out the window. I must have made coffee and drank it. I must have stood and stretched at some point during the day. Several times, probably. I must have stretched several times.

What was I doing the night before? Did I watch TV?

Did I go to bed early? What was on my mind? What was important to me then?

I can no longer recall.

But when it comes to the morning, the morning after I heard the voice, I have detailed memories. In the morning I opened my fridge and took out the bowl of grapes that I'd put there the night before. I ate a grape. It was ice-cold. I pushed it against the roof of my mouth and it burst. And before I left home, before I added my pages to the folder I would give to the ghostwriter, I took the sheet from the stack and folded it four times. I placed it in my pocket. The whole time, all the way to the ghostwriter's office, I knew that I could still change my mind. I could choose at any moment to take the sheet of paper from my pocket, unfold it, and add it to the rest of the pages. I could ask the ghostwriter about the tape when I arrived at his office.

But I don't think it's for the ghostwriter. I think it's for me.

I have seen you. Have you seen me?

The ghostwriter's clients aren't supposed to know I exist. I'm supposed to be secret. Invisible. More invisible than the ghostwriter himself.

Ever since that evening, ever since I heard the whisper, I've had the sense that I'm split in two. That I'm half of me. I've looked at the hand stamping the ticket, holding the strap, pushing open the door, and I've wondered how I can be certain that it really is my hand and not a stranger's. I have seen my reflection in the windows of the train and wondered how I can be sure that it's me I'm seeing. At times I've had the sense that my reflection is flickering, that it goes blurry and then returns to focus. As if somebody were training their camera on me. Ever since I heard that whisper I've had the sense that I am disappearing. I can't explain it better than that.

THEY DON'T MEET AGAIN, NOT AT THE DEPARTMENT STORE café, even though Naomi looks for Laura every time she's there, looks for her coat on one of the hooks or a blond head or a set of pale blue eyes, but she doesn't see her there, which is strange, since she said she goes there all the time. There have been moments when she's thought back to their meeting and wondered if it was all a dream. She's played it over and over in her mind and each time the memory of what they said to each other fades. She's beginning to doubt that it really happened. She repeats Laura's words to herself—it was you who'd become my new life—but she can't hear the sound of Laura's voice, and she's started to forget the details of Laura's face. She tries to recall the face as she stands in front of the mirror in the morning, as her eyeliner pen traces the waterline, as she combs her hair with her little tortoiseshell comb.

Naomi meets Gina for lunch, she folds a piece of wet lettuce into her mouth and chews and chews. Gina is preparing for a trip, a trip that's still quite some time away, and they spend a lot of time talking about the trip's details, not the destination but the journey there. She's concerned about a transfer, a leg of the trip on a small airplane, the kind of airplane people die in—remember that story, the one with the cannibals in the Andes? But you're not flying over the Andes? Also they weren't even cannibals, I mean, technically speaking, sure, they ate human flesh, but it was a question of life and death, and you know, they were devout Catholics ... My passport photo is terrible, I wonder if they'll even let me enter the country ...

Naomi chews and chews. She drinks from her water. Suddenly she wants to say: I had sparkling water recently, I enjoyed it. But it would be an insipid thing to share. She wants to say it to return to the memory. That's clear as day, she's not fooling herself in any way, she's not trying to tell herself anything else: she wants to return to the memory of the encounter, a memory that holds no meaning for Gina. She knows all this and still can't stop herself. She says: I had sparkling water recently, I enjoyed it. She's surprised by the intense pleasure it gives her to speak these meaningless words, to return, alone, to the memory. I want to see her again, Naomi thinks.

She takes the way by the canal to get home. The weather is nice, the ground sparkles, the water is dark, and the air is clear. On a sudden impulse she stops at Rigardi. She takes a seat by the bar. She drinks an espresso. She asks for sweetener, which they don't have, and she doesn't want sugar, so she drinks slowly. If she drinks too fast she'll grimace. She has the sense that her spontaneity will be rewarded somehow. She thinks, It was a sudden impulse that led me to stop here, a feeling that it would be nice to relax with a little coffee for a moment, a little thing I'm doing for myself. She's lying to herself. The reason that she stopped in at Rigardi is that she, upon seeing the café's sign, had a strong feeling that Laura might be there, or that she might appear. For the universe to reward her spontaneity with another encounter she must convince the universe that it really is a spontaneous visit. She stays for a good long while. She looks through a magazine that's been left on the bar counter. One page is earmarked. There's nothing special about this page: makeup ads. Big red mouths and shiny red nails. By the time she leaves Rigardi, darkness has fallen, and she continues on home along the canal, but she doesn't run into Laura on the way.

She goes to the pool, the one she always goes to, the one where she goes twice a week to swim in the long lanes with the very tall ceilings and the changing stalls that line the walls. She changes in the same stall almost every time—as long as it's not taken—locks it, and then sets the red rubber band with the key high up on her arm. As she swims she sometimes worries that the rubber band could slip off, which is why she sets it so high, though she's also had the thought that the rubber band with the key could just as easily snap and sink to the bottom this way. It's not a serious concern. She understands that nothing bad would happen if she lost the key. Worrying is just something to do while she swims, something to think about. Otherwise all there is to occupy her mind is the distance to the person in front of her and the time that's passed since she got into the pool. When she swims one way she sees a big window. When she swims the other way she sees a big clock and an abstract mural with green, blue, and pink fields.

She thinks about the time, and the key.

She climbs out of the pool, showers, gets dressed, and styles her wet hair in front of the little mirror in the changing booth. She pushes it behind her ears, then combs it with oil. She locks the booth with the key and leaves the key in the lock. She walks onto the street.

That's when she sees Laura. That's when she sees Laura's back, her blond hair. She doesn't doubt for a second that this is what she's seeing.

She speeds up to catch her, and the sound of her shoes hitting the pavement with resolute intensity makes Laura turn and look at her with the same expression as the first time, with the same pale fear, before recognition softens her face.

What a coincidence to run into you here, Naomi says. Do you come to swim here? In the pool?

No, I was just passing by. I haven't seen you in so long. What a strange coincidence.

Would you like to have a cup of coffee? Naomi asks. That's all she can manage to say, all she manages right now. What she would like to say is: I've missed you, I've been looking for you, I longed for you.

Laura responds, Yes, I would love to.

They walk back inside, go to the pool cafeteria, just because it's right there. Naomi has the sense that there's no time to lose. The cafeteria smells strongly of chlorine. Laura drinks her coffee black, Naomi stirs the contents of a little pale-blue sachet of sweetener into hers. A small white pill. She says, I'm trying to eat less sugar, but I could never get used to the taste without it, it's been like this since I was a teen, this idea that coffee is undrinkable unless it's sweet. I used to take probably four sugar cubes in my coffee to hide the bitter taste, but I didn't want milk, I thought it would make me seem like a child, I had this feeling that I would only be taken seriously if it looked like I drank my coffee black. Laura smiles and Naomi stops talking. Now she thinks it's the admission itself that makes her seem childish. That she's revealed her preoccupation with what others think about how she takes her coffee, that she still cares even though she's an adult and not a teenager. To reveal that she thinks that's something other people care about. To reveal that she loves sweetness, that she's trying to cut down on sugar, which is to say that she used to eat too much sugar, that she's unable to check her desire for things she should have grown out of long ago.

You think so? Laura says. You think coffee is bitter? I guess it is. I like it, actually. I guess most tastes are acquired.

I guess so, Naomi says.

She stirs her cup with her spoon. She tries to think of something to talk about. But she knows nothing about Laura, doesn't know what interests her, doesn't know what they have in common, doesn't know what she could say that would make Laura take an interest in her.

I was starting to wonder if I'd only dreamed of you, she eventually says.

Why would it have been a dream? Laura asks.

Because it was an unusual encounter, Naomi responds. And because I haven't seen you since then. I was starting to think I'd made it all up. I was trying to remember what you told me when you sat down at my table.

What do you remember? Laura asks.

Naomi looks at her.

Not much, she says, finally. But I really liked talking to you.

I liked talking to you as well, Laura says and looks around the swimming pool's cafeteria, as if she'd spotted a familiar face, before she returns her gaze to Naomi.

I have to go. Let me pay for the coffee. No please, let me.

Laura leaves and Naomi stays at the table, wondering if she said something stupid, if it was a bad idea to ask Laura to have a cup of coffee. She's devastated that she's let the moment slip out of her hands, the moment she's been waiting for, the moment she's fantasized about, their meeting. She's devastated that it's already over, that it will never come back, that she didn't do a better job. She feels as if she's made a serious mistake, but she doesn't know what the mistake is. She feels that her hair, which is still wet, smells of chlorine even though she's washed it, that the smell of chlorine cuts through the oil she's applied to it, that it's got an unpleasant, toxic smell.

Later that week, the second time she goes swimming, she spots Laura again just as she's about to leave. She spots her through the building's glass doors, on the street down the stairs. She sees her walking on and off, sort of aimlessly, as if she were waiting for someone. Her heart races in anticipation. She pulls the door open and walks out. Laura, she says, and Laura looks up. What a coincidence to run into you here. You're out for a walk?

Yes, I was just passing by. What a strange coincidence. Would you like to get a drink?

Yes, Laura says. I know a place.

She takes Naomi to Rigardi. So I was right, Naomi thinks, with a heady feeling that she's about to meet her fate. Her powerful conviction the other day, that sense that she might run into Laura at Rigardi, it did mean something. She knew, she knew something without knowing it. There is magic in the world, she thinks, and life is vast and great. She sees herself in the mirror behind the bar, and she looks at Laura, who is looking at her.

There are not a lot of people at the bar. They hang their coats on the same hook. They each order a little glass of wine. They get to know each other.

When Laura listens to Naomi, she lets her take the time she needs to find her words.

I've never really put down roots in this city, Naomi says, though I've lived here for a long time. But what would that look like, putting down roots? I'm not sure, to be honest. I can't complain. I've lived in the same apartment for many years, and it's not that expensive. I have friends. I have a job I like.

Doing what?

I'm a station hostess, says Naomi.

Station hostess? Laura asks.

Yes, a station hostess, at the radio. A classical music station.

I know that station. But what does a station hostess do? Laura asks. I don't know what that means.

Naomi says no, and she laughs, and she says, It's a

pretty name for a job that's not very glamorous. I take care of the people who work there, like a kind of secretary. I know their names and I know when their shows are aired and I make sure that things are in their right places, and I do little things like distributing the mail and making coffee and putting out water pitchers. And on Fridays, when there's a live concert at the radio house, I take care of the audience.

Is that annoying, Laura says, working on Friday evenings?

It's not that annoying, Naomi says, no, it's not so bad. I like being there. The radio house is beautiful.

I've never been to the radio house, Laura says. I'd like to see it.

You must have seen it, Naomi says, it's in the middle of the city, close to the museum of natural history. You must have walked by. You don't necessarily notice it if you don't know what it is, it's not flashy but it's very beautiful inside. I'll try to keep an eye out next time I'm in the area, Laura says. I always listen to that station. It's good company. I probably know the programming by heart. I would love to have a job like that. Have you worked there for a long time?

Naomi smiles, flattered by her interest.

Yes, she says, I have worked there for a long time. I ended up there by chance. I'd done a year at the university—this was after the department store—I was planning to become an interpreter, and then I got that job for the summer, and after the summer they asked me to stay on full-time, and I couldn't say no. I don't regret it. I don't think I would have been a good interpreter.

She takes a sip of the wine, which is a light red wine.

Do you have siblings? Laura asks. Yes, Naomi says. Two brothers. I'm the youngest. We're quite far apart in age. The eldest was almost fifteen when I was born and the other was eight. I often felt like an only child.

Those are big age gaps, Laura says.

Do you have siblings? Naomi asks, and Laura seems to hesitate before she responds.

No. I don't have any siblings. It was always just me. I've always been alone.

She takes a sip of her wine. Her brown lipstick leaves a subtle, half-moon-shaped mark.

Have you ever fantasized, Naomi asks, about having a twin you don't know about?

Laura looks blankly at her.

No, she says, that thought has never struck me.

When we met, Naomi says, you said you had the sense that there were two of you.

Yes, Laura says, but not like a twin. Twins aren't the same person.

You're right, Naomi says. But how do you think you'd react if you saw someone who looked just like you? Someone you'd never met?

Laura considers the question.

I'd be scared, she says. And I wouldn't believe my eyes.

Naomi takes a big sip of her light red wine, a big and eager sip.

I read something in the paper, she says, this was a long time ago. I read about a pair of twins who were separated at birth. Neither knew the other existed. They were Americans, they'd grown up on opposite sides of the country, several time zones apart. It wasn't until their twenties that they ended up in the same city, by coincidence.

Laura listens attentively as Naomi talks. She follows the movement of her lips, she looks at the shiny teeth, the red tongue, the dark eyes.

It was a big city, Naomi says. I don't remember which one, but a big city. They could have lived their whole lives there without ever meeting, no problem. But then, one day, they spotted each other—and they saw each other at the same time—they saw each other in the subway, one of them going down the escalator and the other going up. Both of them described it as a dream. Yes, it was like a dream, that's what they said. And they said it later, too, after they had properly met, after they had talked to each other, that it was like a dream, that it was like meeting someone you'd known your whole life, and at the same time—I love this expression—they felt like perfect strangers. Isn't that beautiful? Being a perfect stranger?

She falters, because she suddenly understands that she's stopped talking about the American twins and started to talk about Laura and herself, and she both hopes and fears that Laura will understand, too. Maybe, she thinks, we belong together in some mysterious way. Maybe we have the same soul. Maybe we're the same person. Maybe you were right the first time we saw each other. Maybe I am your new life.

Laura looks into her eyes, and Naomi notices that Laura's pupils are very small.

I suppose so, Laura says. I suppose it's beautiful. It's not anything I've ever thought of before.

She drinks from her wine, careful to place her lips right on the half-moon mark from her lipstick.

There's a triangle-shaped ashtray in white, red, and blue on the bar counter. CINZANO. For a moment they're silent.

Where did you grow up? Naomi asks.

Laura looks at her with an expression she can't decipher, and she wonders if she's said too much. She doesn't look upset, not exactly. Not sad, either. No, it's more as if Laura is nonplussed, absolutely nonplussed by the question. She seems surprised, Naomi thinks, surprised in a way that's not in proportion to the question itself, and it seems as if she can't figure out how to answer, as if she has to think about what she can or wants to share, and has to consider it carefully, very carefully.

Have you ever eaten a perfectly fresh peach? Laura says, finally.

From the tree? I don't know if I've ever seen a peach tree, Naomi says.

They've got pink blossoms, Laura says.

Yes, Naomi says. Now that you say that I do think I've seen peach blossoms. I've seen peach branches. They sell them at the market in springtime.

The peaches you buy in the grocery store, Laura says, those are soft like suede. But a peach you pluck from the tree is nothing like that. No.

She casts a brief glance at the ashtray, frowning.

I grew up in a house with peaches in the garden, she says, with a slightly distant, mechanical voice. The branches reached all the way up to my bedroom window. In the summer I could open my window and put out a hand to pluck a peach. They were all downy. Your whole mouth would fill with down when you took a bite.

Naomi pictures the house, the window and the vines and the fruit, but she's not able to picture Laura as a child, and when she tries to picture her biting into a peach, the fruit just looks like the peaches she's used to, smooth and soft like suede. It's the only kind of peach she's seen, the only kind of peach she's able to imagine. She can't picture what Laura is telling her.

Laura falls silent again, absentmindedly poking the stem of her wineglass.

Generally I don't like to dwell on the past, she says. Do you?

No, Naomi says. I don't, really.

I prefer to think of the future, Laura says. It's so full of possibilities.

Yes, Naomi says.

All the versions of life that haven't happened yet, that are just waiting for us.

Naomi smiles.

But you can't live all those different versions of life, she says. We only have one single life, after all.

You think so? Laura says. I can't bear that thought.

Naomi doesn't know how to respond.

Another glass of wine?

No, Laura says. No, I have to go.

It's dark outside, cold, but inside it's warm and red. I'll stay for a bit, Naomi says, and she watches Laura's back as she leaves, her blond hair, the hand that pulls the door open, the door that shuts.

She's always the one leaving me, Naomi thinks. Sometime I would like to be the first to leave. But even more than that—yes, more than anything—I'd like her to stay.

A week goes by. Then two. Naomi goes swimming, she goes twice a week as always, but she doesn't see Laura on the street outside. She changes and gets dressed quickly, and then she lingers inside the glass doors of the pool, watching the street and extending the time that Laura, by sheer coincidence, might pass by, but they don't run into each other. Feeling exposed, she thinks to herself that she's being punished for her superstition.

Naomi goes to the department store, the beauty section, it's a relaxing moment to herself, she looks at the perfumes and the makeup, she doesn't buy anything. She takes the escalator upstairs. She hangs up her coat and looks for Laura's coat on one of the hooks, but it's not there. She drinks a cup of coffee. She waits for Laura to appear, but Laura doesn't appear.

She soon begins, again, to ask herself if it really happened, if they really met, if it was all a dream.

She knows she's got a vivid imagination.

Perhaps, she thinks—she entertains herself with this thought, she doesn't take it seriously—I should go to Rigardi and ask if they've seen me there with a blond woman.

But in truth she knows she doesn't need to. She knows it wasn't a dream. It's no longer difficult for her to picture the details of Laura's face, it's very easy, she doesn't need to close her eyes, doesn't need to make an effort. She knows that they really did meet. That they did speak to each other. That Laura exists, somewhere. She knows it's only happenstance, an unlucky happenstance instead of the lucky chance that brought them together, that's made it so that it's soon three weeks since they saw each other.

In some moments she knows this, and at other times she is equally convinced that it's not at all by happenstance that she no longer runs into Laura; that Laura, instead, avoids her, that Laura has changed up the way she moves through the city, that she doesn't want to run into her, that Naomi makes her ill at ease. Naomi argues with herself. It's always Laura who has to leave. It's always she who decides when their encounter is over. But that time she sat down at my table, that was her approaching me, wasn't it? She started it, didn't she? It was she who walked into my life, wasn't it? Me taking her coat, that was happenstance, that was me, but the fact that she came up to my table, she did that willingly. She saw me. I was the one who made her shy.

Naomi goes to see Karol, she's at his house, and they play with Lou, and Lou makes her a drawing of all three of them, but the child is unhappy with the results and tears up the paper. Karol asks what's going on in Naomi's life and at first she's about to respond sincerely, about to tell him that all she's been able to think about lately is when she'll run into a stranger, a woman about whom she knows almost nothing, not where she lives, not what she does for work, not what her phone number is, nothing at all other than the fact that her name is Laura and she's got no siblings, that she grew up in a house with a garden and peach trees and that she was recently left by somebody, but instead she says, No, you know what my life is like, nothing happens, but I don't have anything to complain about, either. Lou makes a new drawing, and this time it's a success, Naomi can take it home with her, thanks so much. It's a red drawing, the thin drafting paper is crowded with red scratches, hard scratches, and in a few places the wet marker has bored through the paper. What is it? she asks. Don't you see? Lou says. It's you. She smiles and says, Yes, I see, of course, just like me. She asks Karol if he's ever eaten a peach straight from the tree. No, he replies, I don't think so. I've barely seen a peach growing on trees. Me neither, she replies. Do they grow this far north? We've got apricots, of course, Karol says pensively, and Naomi says, But that's not the same fruit at all. Larissa comes home, she's got a paper bag in her arms that she sets down on the floor—So dark in here—and she drops her keys and flicks on the ceiling light, and Lou demonstratively squints and puts up a hand. Naomi, Larissa says, I haven't seen you in ages, are you staying for dinner? No, Naomi says, I really need to leave. But you'll stay for a glass of wine at least, won't you? Sure, why not. The kitchen is modern, black and red, and on the counter is a bouquet of mint in a drinking glass, and she looks at Lou's little hand, hard at work with the drawings, and she drinks her wine while Karol cooks, and Larissa sits down across from her and says, This time of year I just want to go somewhere, it's so dark and dreary, it feels like it's been winter for half a year at this point, I don't think I can stand it anymore, I actually can't stand it any longer. Did you hear about Gina's trip? She's so neurotic, afraid of flying I think, no it's not that, she's not afraid of dying in an airplane accident, but she's scared of those small planes, she's scared of being stranded like those cannibals in the Andes. She's obsessed with that story. I don't think we should call them cannibals actually, it's disrespectful, it was a question of survival, it's not exactly as if they'd been walking around with dreams of eating one another. It's so like her to complain about the plane when she's lucky to travel somewhere sunny and warm. I'd gladly swap places with her. What's she doing there anyway? It's a mystery to me, too—a strange place to visit. I don't remember. She told me, but I don't remember. We'll have to ask her. Karol, I'm going to open the window actually, it gets so smoky in here otherwise. Sweetheart, I love that, why don't you write your name, too, and today's date? Let me help you. Have you ever eaten a peach straight from the tree? A peach? No, I don't think I have. Karol said the same thing. Yes, I don't even know if I've seen a peach tree, have you? I was saying, of course we've got apricots here, but that's a different fruit altogether. I think they've got peaches farther south, but maybe we've got them in the south here, too, they might be able to grow there. It's not common, in any case. But you know, when we go on summer vacation, we'll sometimes find figs there, yeah, there was this big, sturdy tree, I've actually never seen that up here before, it's got to be something unique about the climate right there. Are you going this summer? We'll see, we'll have to see. I feel that it's gotten too expensive. The owners raised the rent even though the house is exactly the same, and there's barely even a functioning toilet, so I think it's a bit too steep actually, kind of unreasonable, honestly. But it's gotten so touristy that I'm sure there are ten people on the wait list ready to bankrupt themselves in that hovel. Come on, don't say that, it's not a hovel, it's just too expensive for us, that's all, and we want to spend our money elsewhere. I'd love to have my own house at some point. Yes. Wouldn't you? Lou, would you like a glass of milk? Do you want to come sit with us? Are you sure you don't want to stay for dinner, Naomi? Karol always makes too much food anyway. It's okay, thank you, really, I'm just about to leave. Ah, I'm an idiot, you don't eat meat. It's totally fine, I'm not eating anyway, seriously I'm fine, thank you, I'm about to leave anyway. It's getting late. What else is happening in your life, Naomi? We hardly ever see you. You need to come by more often. We'll have to invite you over for dinner, a proper dinner, and make something you can eat.

Oh, Naomi says, I just told Karol, nothing much happens in my life, but I've got nothing to complain about, either.

She gets off the train at the station with the yellow tiles. It's got tall ceilings and there's a newspaper kiosk and benches in yellow hard plastic. An echo makes the voices of the waiting passengers round and turbid, they bleed into the signals, into the loudspeaker's female voice. The doors to the train shut behind her with a loud slam and she hears, faintly, the sound of a busker's accordion. Lambada.

She decides to take the street by the canal. She deliberates for a brief moment, collects herself, weighs hope against the risk of being disappointed, and then she walks into Rigardi. The bartender has on a ball cap with the text DADDY'S LITTLE DADDY. She looks at her own reflection in the mirror behind the bar and takes off her coat, letting it hang over her bare arm. She orders a little glass of wine. She looks around, scanning the crowd for a familiar face, seeing the slot machine blinking in the dark, and then there's a cool hand on her shoulder. What a coincidence to run into you here.

She looks into Laura's pale eyes, her very small pupils, her mouth where the brown lipstick has congealed somewhat, her face that's so pale against her black clothes—the same clothes, Naomi realizes, that she was wearing the last time they saw each other. Laura also has her coat thrown over her arm, but she holds on to it with the other hand, almost desperately.

Have you been here long? Laura says.

No, Naomi says, no, I just came. I haven't seen you in forever. Now she realizes that Laura is, in fact, unusually pale. I haven't seen you, either, I haven't seen you, even though I've been looking for you. Oh, you have? Yes, I've been looking for you, but I haven't seen you anywhere. How incredible, Naomi says, that we came here tonight, both of us. I hadn't even planned to come here, I just happened to be nearby, I was just walking by on my way home, I had an impulse. Just think, chance brought us together again.

Laura doesn't respond. Her mouth is wide, brown, tense, and closed.

Do you want to leave? Naomi says. I want to leave with you. I want you to come home with me.

Laura leaves with her.

They take a short walk in the dry, ice-cold air. Laura doesn't have gloves on and her hands are red. Naomi takes her hands in her own. To warm them, she says. It smells like fire. She blows on Laura's hands, she presses her thumb into Laura's soft palm. They walk on the sidewalk, they swerve for people coming toward them. The traffic lights create green and red tracks in the canal and the taxicabs drive past with their signs lit, cars with shiny black windows. The sounds of their shoes hitting the asphalt create one single, rhythmic cadence. Laura's heart is beating hard.

Naomi pushes the door to her building open and leads the way up, all five sets of stairs. She holds Laura's hand the entire way, fearing that the other woman might—if she let go for just one moment—disappear, turn on her heel and run away. She doesn't know where it comes from, this feeling that they need to hurry, that what is happening is very important, urgent, but the feeling is thrilling, it makes her feel excited and alive, and on the landing they need to stop, just for a moment, to catch their breath.

She unlocks the door and lets Laura enter first before she steps inside, shuts the door behind them, and locks it from the inside. In the darkness they take each other's hands. Laura, I missed you, I longed for you, where have you been? Laura smiles, and her smile is tired. I missed you, too, she says. I really did. I'm sorry. It seems I've been looking for you in the wrong places entirely.

Naomi lets go of Laura's hands and turns on the light. She gets a bottle of white wine and two glasses, she says, I don't want to waste any time, I wanted to be alone with you. I haven't been able to stop thinking about you.

The wine isn't as chilled as it should be, but it doesn't matter. Laura drinks a little.

We're not strangers anymore, she says.

No, Naomi says, we aren't strangers anymore. So what are we, then? Are we friends?

I don't know what to call it, Laura says. Not strangers. That's enough for me.

She kisses Naomi, and her tongue is soft and rough, her teeth are hard and slippery. Laura shuts her eyes.

It's windy outside, she says. Isn't it windy outside?

Yes, Naomi says, and her sweet breath hits Laura's cheek, it's always loud here when it's windy outside, I think it's because I live on the top floor, it howls like a full storm. And there's the tree, too, in the yard.

Laura opens her pale eyes.

Did you know that the word pupil comes from the Latin word for doll? Naomi says.

I didn't know that, Laura says.

That's because you see your own reflection like a little doll when you look another person in the eye.

It's true, Laura says, and Naomi looks into Laura's pupils, into her own very small eyes, and laughs at the reflection's doll face. Her nose looks abnormally large.

The eye's curve makes the proportions of the face look strange, like a funhouse mirror.

Do you know the difference between love and obsession? Naomi asks.

No, Laura says.

And the difference between obsession and desire?

No, Laura says, I don't know.

Naomi kisses her, once, and she thinks that it's like kissing herself. Her tongue is rough, her teeth are hard and slippery. She shuts her eyes. She opens her eyes again. It's strange to be this close to another person, close enough to be a doll in her eyes, and at the same time not strange at all. It's as natural as breathing. It isn't difficult. She touches Laura's cheek, and it's not difficult. But as she touches her cheek, when that is happening in real life, she has the chilling sensation that they're not alone. Not that another person is in the apartment, but that there's someone else in Laura's thoughts.

Laura, she asks, who was it who left you?

Laura backs away, far enough that Naomi loses her reflection. Now she no longer sees herself.

I can't tell you that, Laura says. I don't want to.

Naomi is unable to respond. She knows, deep inside she knows that there's nothing she can say, that she shouldn't say anything, though she wants to keep asking: Who was it? Do you still think about her? Do you miss her? Have you seen her since, at a distance or close-up? Do you wish it had never happened? Do you wish that I were she? Are you going to compare us to each other? Will the comparison be to her advantage?

Do I have any chance of winning? Are you going to want me more than you want her to take you back?

Her tongue is dry from the wine and her temples throb in despair and in shame of having brought up the subject, shame of her own interest in Laura, shame of her own hunger for Laura's history, her own desire to insert herself into that history. It's too early to make such claims, and perhaps it will never be time to make them. Perhaps she's ruined her chance to get close to Laura by demanding closeness too fast, too early.

It was someone I trusted, Laura says.

The words swell slightly in the air between them. Laura softens and removes a strand of hair from the corner of her mouth before she caresses Naomi's hair, which is slick with oil.

I don't like to dwell on the past, she says. I prefer to think of the future. Don't you?

And back then there was nowhere near the kind of tourism they've got there now, it was quite pastoral, yes, simple, and other than the family in the house next door we would be essentially all alone throughout the summer, and the fishermen, though they kept to themselves...that's how I remember it...that's how I remember it...

There's a particular way of describing the sky that I've often wondered about, that I've never understood—a way of describing the color of the sky—and that is *azure blue*! What does that mean, really? I used to read it in novels, "The sky was azure blue." *Azure* ... I suppose to me it sounds like some kind of stone, and I guess maybe that's what it means. Blue like a...some sort of very blue stone. Azure blue. But the blue of the sky, no, that to me is a different kind of blue, it's not a hard blue, like a stone, but a type of soft blue, isn't it, one that sort of enfolds you! Yes! It's a soft blue! I want, if I can make a note, if you don't mind... I'd prefer it if you didn't write *azure blue*! That would be wrong. I don't want that! Now, in any case...I forget what I was...What I'm trying

to say is that on this day—I remember this—
the sky was very, very blue, it was deeply blue,
and still bright, yes, it was a day with a very
particular kind of blue, blue sky...

It still happens that I come across little things
from that other life, and every time... every
time... every time it's as if I'm unprepared,
even though... yes, I guess I simply forget
sometimes that that life is done, or rather
I don't think about it at all and then I'm reminded... not so much of the past, but of
something else, the future that's been lost...
and now I live in the future, what used to be
the future, though what I'm saying is... this
was not... this was not how I pictured the future! No... no, it was different. Yes, it was. I
had pictured something else. Not that I've got
anything to complain about! No... that's not
what I'm saying. I'm not saying that what I
imagined was better. Just... different...

It was some time, it only happened once, and
I can't have been old—I imagine it was, it must
have been that summer when we went...
we went... well, I'll get to that later, I'll come
back to it—it was the same summer, though
earlier, I know that much—which means it
must have been in June. June of that year. Yes.

That's when they came, my dad's...my father's brother...my uncle...and his wife. Why did they come? Ah! I know! They were there to babysit us! That's right. My parents were going somewhere, on their own, or perhaps it was—was it just Mother? At least I remember it this way, that it was an unusual event, my uncle and his wife coming to visit, and they were...right, that must have been it, my parents were traveling. That must have been it, because they were in charge, my uncle and his wife, yes. Exactly. That's right. Because that's the whole memory. It was...and I can't have been old. No. If it's true that it was that summer, and I think it must have been, then I was just four years old, about to turn five. Right. I'll tell you about it. What happened was...so, we were all sitting down to eat. Yes. Exactly. And I was in my usual chair. And my uncle and his wife...yes, we were all eating there. And it was...I saw...suddenly I saw...it was an amazingly...what a banal thing to notice! But suddenly I saw, I saw how my uncle's wife... I could have called her *aunt*, but we were never close like that...they never came to visit again and we never went to...Anyway, so she was holding...Wait, how was it again... she held the silverware, or maybe she put it down...or it could have been the way she cut her food? She did—well, it doesn't matter... ah, but there's a detail—something she did! I must remember what it was she did exactly. Because what I do remember is...yes, what I do remember...is that in that moment I understood something...it was the first time...and there was no going back after...I understood it as if in one fell swoop, after I'd seen her...the way she did...and that it was different...that they were different from us, and we were different from them. I understood, yes, for some reason this was what made me understand that my parents had left something, and that there was a place, over there, somewhere, where they did things differently.

My family owns a chocolate factory, we've always been in the praline industry, as long as there is cacao that is going to be our lot in life. And our specialty, the crowning glory, our showpiece, is a little chocolate praline filled with persipan—no, not marzipan, but *persipan*!

All the women in my family weep the same way. That was something I realized early on. My mother...my daughter...my aunt—yes, on both sides! We weep suddenly and loudly...it's a different thing with the men! Ah, I come from a family of weeping men! I love it! We're a family of weepers...all of us...yes, we love to weep in my family, weeping comes easily to us... The men, they cry quietly and voluminously, they wipe their tears discreetly... Sometimes I'd turn to my father—at a concert, for instance—and his face would be all wet with tears, though I hadn't heard a sound. With my mother, or my aunt, it was... no... they would have had to leave the auditorium! It was like a coughing fit when they cried! They were able to hold it in for most of the concert, but then, suddenly, it just came, like a full-on scream, a veritable attack! Yes, I remember this clearly from when I was a child. I wasn't a weeper myself back then, not in that way... I must have cried, the way all children cry... but I had not yet acquired this strange way of crying, the way the women in my family weep. When did I do that, then? When did it happen for the first time? Well, I'll have to try to remember...

I PICK UP THIS WEEK'S CASSETTE TAPES FROM THE GHOST-
writer. We drink a little cup of coffee. We smoke a little cigarette.

I haven't told him about the whisper.

I get home and get to work.

I listen.

I've never seen the ghostwriter's clients. I've never seen what they look like. They only exist as voices inside of me. Once or twice, if I've gotten attached to a particular woman's voice, I've asked the ghostwriter what they look like. Some of the women have pleasant voices. Others have unusual voices. Strangely deep, or girlish. In those cases I want to know what face corresponds to the voice, if the voice has its counterpart in the face I've been picturing. There are some voices that make me dream, that make me fantasize.

The ghostwriter never wants to tell me what they look like. He refuses. He doesn't think it's something I should care about. The women and I are not supposed to ever meet. They're not supposed to know I exist. They're not supposed to find out that anyone other than him handles the material that makes up their life. It's about trust. It's important that the women can talk about their lives without wondering what someone might think and feel about what they describe, without thinking about anyone other than the ghostwriter. Without thinking about me. I am a pair of ears, I am a pair of hands. No more, no less. I am transformed into every woman as I type. Their words enter one part of my body and exit through another. I am to type as if it concerned my own life. When I type the words of the women they also become my words. We are, in the moment I listen and type, the same person.

And I am to write down what I hear without distractions. I am not supposed to know anything about the women other than what they tell me. I am not to picture them, not to be moved by anything they say. The ghostwriter has told me that if I believe I recognize someone's voice, if I believe that it belongs to someone I've met in real life, someone I've met in my own life, someone I know, I must immediately stop typing.

This has never happened so far.

But what if one of them had seen me?

If one of them wanted something from me?

Ever since I heard the whisper I've kept the piece of paper with the transcription in my pocket. I check on it sometimes. I want to ensure that it's still there.

I have seen you. Have you seen me?

I really did hear those words. I always write down exactly what I hear.

Ever since I heard the whisper I've been unable to think of anything else while I listen, unable to think of anything other than when I'll hear it again, when I'll hear it the next time. The first few seconds of listening to a new cassette tape I'm expectant and terrified, and when I hear the voice that begins to speak—a clear voice, a clear voice describing a life, the voice of a person speaking to everybody and no one, speaking to herself—I feel both relief and disappointment. I work quickly so that I can move on. I listen to the next recording, and the next.

But I don't hear the whisper, I don't hear the whisper again, and there's no new clue.

It smells like fire, BANG, and I travel through the darkness. It's morning but it looks like night, I've got my pages in a paper folder. I press it against my chest. I'm tired. I look at the other passengers in the car and I see their reflections in the windows, I rest my gaze somewhere, on a window, on a face, I see them read CITY, I see them stare out the windows. When I get off at the station by the ghostwriter's office it's still dark. The ground sparkles. I walk past the grocery store signs, which are red and garish, they call to me: SALE! I walk past the laundromat and the bakery, I smell the scent of bread and detergent. I see the basement window to the ghostwriter's office. The window is dirty. I see, through the window, the ghostwriter's back where he sits at his desk. I pause for a second with my folder pressed to my chest. I walk down the steps and push the heavy door open.

Quite windy yesterday, the ghostwriter says. But today is a beautiful day.

We smoke a cigarette. Dawn breaks outside his basement window.

Today is a beautiful day, I say.

I give him my pages. We have a good working relationship. The ghostwriter wants to talk to me about a few of the women, go over a few of my transcriptions, ask a few questions. When I leave it's already getting close to lunch.

I buy a cup of coffee and a croissant in the station kiosk. The croissant is plain. I stir sugar into the hot coffee with a wooden stick. When I'm done I toss the stirrer on the ground. The ground is covered in cigarette butts, bird shit, and spit. The coffee tastes sweet and delicious. It's true what the ghostwriter said. Today is a beautiful day.

I go to the department store. I stand outside for a moment. I collect myself. Then I push open the heavy doors and step inside. The department store is all beige marble, chrome, and mirrors. It's warm inside. I unbutton my coat. I head to the beauty section. I look at the lipsticks. I try all the brown shades on the back of my hand. The lipsticks have women's names: BETTY, JUDY, DIANE, VERONIQUE. My hand is covered in brown lines. I don't find what I want. Not quite the brown shade I'm looking for.

I ride the escalator to the top floor and take a seat in the department store café. I drink an espresso, I eat a little chocolate praline. Persipan. It's free. It's included in the price of a coffee. I rub a white napkin on the back of my hand to remove the lipstick. Pale lines remain. My hands are dry. I almost doze off in the department store café, where the sounds are muted. I like it here. I forget about time. It's impossible to know what time of day it is when you're in the department store. The light is the same all the time.

Eventually I stand up and leave. The sun has set and I

walk home along the canal. The mud has frozen and the streetlights cause the frost to glitter.

When I get home I draw a bath. I'm cold. I pour oil into the water and the oil makes the water look like thin milk. I get the bottle of sparkling water from the fridge and pour myself a glass. That's all there's left in the bottle. One glass. I put on the radio and slip in the bath to warm up. I've left the bathroom door open so that I can hear the radio. I sink down to escape the chilly air that enters through the doorway.

I take a sip of water and hold it in my mouth before I swallow. The contrast between the warm, smooth bathwater and the cold, fizzy drinking water is delicious.

I listen to the radio.

I close my eyes and imagine that I'm a glamorous woman enjoying a bath.

Later, when I'm in the dark, warm and soft after the bath, I think about the whisper.

I have seen you. Have you seen me?

When I wake up I don't have work. I go to the nearby café. Rigardi. The floor inside is checkered in red and white, the sun streams in through the vaulted windows, and there is a mirror behind the bar. I drink an espresso. I spend some time reading CITY. I lean against the counter. I lean my arms on it. It's warm from the sun. Rigardi is warm, even though it's so cold outside. My espresso cup has an ear without a hole and I hold it with my thumb and pointer finger, pinching hard so I don't drop it when I bring it to my mouth. I drink carefully to avoid burning my tongue. I lick my lips. Away from the windows, the slot machines are blinking, and behind the slot machines is a double-swinging door in lacquered, reddish wood with a brass-framed window, like on a boat.

I pay. I receive my change.

Then I walk along the canal.

In the daytime the thought of the whisper doesn't bother me. The idea that somebody has seen me doesn't trouble me.

There are lots of people who see me every day. Lots of people I see, too. There are lots of people who see me without ever learning anything about me. Without ever learning my name. Without learning when I was born. Without knowing what I think about or what I've experienced. There could be people who've seen me every day for years and we're still strangers. It's the way it's supposed to be. That's what it's like to live in a big city. We're never alone, and we don't know each other.

I never felt alone before I heard the whisper.

I never thought about it before.

It was close one time. Yes, once I did get close. Close call, I almost put everything on the line. I realized, and maybe he realized, too ... I will never know ... but I didn't do it. I couldn't. I turned around and went back home. And when I was walking home by the canal, that's when I heard something that made me look—it was a busker, but I couldn't see who was playing, I just heard the sound that made me look. I can't explain this in any rational way. I can't. I'll leave that task to you. You'll have to explain it in a way that makes sense. But I turned, because of the music, and I looked back, so I was facing the direction I'd come from, which was his direction ... and I saw ... yes, I *felt* it in that moment, I felt it with every fiber in my body! That there are things we can't say out loud to each other!

I really wasn't feeling well that day, there was something going on already in the morning when I woke up, and of course we'd been drinking the night before and got to bed pretty late, so at first I thought ... it was that kind of *quivering* anxiety, when you're all ... something that just staggers and, how do you say, *tears* through your chest, just wreaking havoc, yes, that's what it felt like, and I had a headache, too. Yes. Classic, of course. I drank some water but then I thought, no, you know what, I don't think... I actually do think I'm sick. And it was as if... it was like magic when I had that thought, or how should I put it, perhaps the opposite, some kind of dark magic, because then I lie down to rest for a moment, to get over the headache, and I probably took a painkiller, too, and then—it was as if I was possessed, I was just shaking. What I mean is, suddenly I had the shivers, I lay there and I was shaking and I was hot and cold all at once and I thought, Oh sweet Jesus, what's happening to me... I've always been a bit of a hypochondriac, but when something like this happens it's as if everything just shuts down. I was all... and then I had diarrhea. But after that I was able to sleep, for a moment at least I slept, quite deeply I would say, and then I woke up and I actually did feel better, not exactly top-notch but much better and more, well, better than when I woke up the first time, actually. It just blew over. It was so odd. And then, what could it have been, probably no more than an hour later... here you might think... ah, I don't know... perhaps it's silly to think this way...

For as long as I can remember... I've always wanted to begin a story that way. Yes, that's how I want this story to start. The story of my life. For as long as I can remember ... the problem is just the continuation. The problem is just the remembering. It's hard to do it like this, how can I put it, on command ... I've always found it difficult to talk about myself. But here I am, paying good money to do exactly that, so I guess I just need to grin and bear it, right? It's like being in therapy. Something I've never done. It seems like a waste of money to me. To sit there and go on about yourself while some unfortunate soul has to listen. No thanks. Not for me. For as long as I can ... how can I put this. Okay. I really wish there were something, anything, in my life that I could say that about. For as long as I remember I have—but I can't think of anything. Well, that's one way to begin, of course. For as long as I can remember I have ... For as long as I can remember I've wanted to start a story in this way: For as long as I can remember. And then it goes from there. With something interesting. Something about me. For as long as I can remember. Yes, why not begin there. How far back can I remember? How far ... I'm trying to think. My first memory. Always the same problem. I've ... yes. I've seen pictures ... photographs. Right. Once upon a time I believed in reincarnation. Because I had this very strong memory of having worn clothes, the kinds of clothes that people wore in the past, and I had this memory of being in the countryside, which I imagined was a memory from a past life. It wasn't a clear memory at all, not at all. It was just a ...a feeling...those itchy clothes and this wet grass, I remember that, and I was outdoors ... and I grew up in the city—I'll get to that later, I'll make a note to get back to that, my childhood, in the city—I barely left the city at all before I was a teenager, barely saw a tree before I was...but this memory was so, so strong, and I was certain it had somehow followed me from a previous life and into the one I'm living now. I was absolutely sure. And it was a comfort to me, this belief in reincarnation ... perhaps that specific part in particular, the idea that you could bring a memory into the next life. Because that's the terrible thing about being reborn... if you believe that kind of thing...that you can live again, but not bring anything with you ... though I stopped believing in it, because I got to see a photograph, a photo of myself at four or five years old. And I was wearing a costume! I was wearing a costume... which was those old clothes. And god knows why I remembered grass, wet grass, since there was no grass in that picture, I'll have you know... For as long as I can remember I have believed in reincarnation. No, that's not true, it's not. I can't say that. But how nice it would be if I still did! The story could have started that way!

SOON IT SEEMS LIKE THE MOST NATURAL THING IN THE world that Laura is in Naomi's home, that she's at the kitchen table with Naomi in the morning, sitting with the open newspaper and the coffee cups and the oranges and the egg cup with the eggshells at the bottom, with the radio that's on and the sun that comes through the window, the dust hovering in the light. When Naomi has dressed and left the house, Laura is still there. She washes her hair with Naomi's shampoo, uses Naomi's perfume, puts on Naomi's clothes. The clothes are a little tight. Laura is slightly taller than Naomi and a little wider, but they fit, she's able to pull up the zippers and button the shirts. She's put her lipstick in the bathroom cabinet; she wants Naomi to feel free to use it.

One morning Naomi does try the lipstick, but she concludes that it doesn't suit her. It makes her look a little pale, just as it does Laura. A difficult shade. She spots a white hair as she removes the lipstick with a cotton round in front of the mirror. She pulls it out.

Laura likes being in Naomi's home. She likes the big kitchen window, her plants, the bookcases in the hall, the CD collection and the stereo, the leather armchairs, the white Bakelite telephone, the poster in the living room: a black-and-white photograph of a skinny woman emerging from the shadows, TANZTHEATER WUPPERTAL. She likes the low bed. Naomi doesn't have nightstands, but there's a lamp on the floor and an alarm clock, and a jar with thick marigold salve, and sometimes Naomi will put her earrings next to these things if she's forgotten to take them out before they go to bed. Laura's side has nothing. She's not brought anything into Naomi's home, nothing other than the clothes she's wearing, and the lipstick.

She opens the greasy lid of the cream jar and moisturizes her knuckles, then smells them. She reads the salve's list of ingredients. She turns on the radio in the kitchen. You make your own fun. While she waits for Naomi's arrival, which is the same time every evening, time stretches into a long, taut string.

Often she just sits in one of the armchairs, idle, waiting.

Naomi spends her days savoring the knowledge that someone is waiting for her at home.

She adds grounds and water to the coffeemaker and chats with Felix for a bit. Naomi, he says, you're always dressed as if you're going somewhere, I always hear you coming down the hallway in your tall boots and it's a lovely sound. Today is chilly, isn't it? But as long as the air is dry, it's manageable. You just wrap your scarf a little tighter. When it's wet and cold, though, that's when it's unbearable, don't you think? Still, spring can't come quickly enough. I wish I could have a cup of coffee, but I can't do it anymore, a cup in the morning is fine but even one more and I'll be tossing and turning all night. Ah, I wanted to tell you, I read such a funny little book this weekend. I found it at a flea market, you know, one of those funky little markets where they sell all manner of junk, old photos, bits and bobs, and I found this book—I don't remember how much I paid, wasn't much in any case, they were basically giving it away for free—and then I couldn't put it down all weekend. It was very strange. I'll lend it to you. Remind me and I'll bring it to the office.

She takes a little walk through the radio building's park on her lunch break. The park has a pond and benches that are screwed to the ground. It's not open to the general public, only the radio's employees, and nobody goes there to enjoy the scenery.

She smokes a little cigarette with Anne.

She's not told anyone about Laura, and now that Laura has moved in with her it seems too late. Maybe she won't tell anyone ever. Maybe she doesn't have to. Maybe she no longer needs anyone else in her life. There's nobody she'd like to tell about Laura. It's true, she has no great desire to share Laura with the rest of the world, there's no person she'd like to introduce Laura to. She's got no desire to have Laura meet her friends, no desire to have Laura meet her family, no desire to show Laura any glimpse of who she was before they met. That version of her has come to seem incomplete and pointless. That version of her would threaten their happiness. That version frightens her the same way she's frightened by the thought of who Laura was before they met. Why should Laura love a version of her that she's never met and never will meet? Why should Laura love a version of her who's never met Laura, who doesn't love Laura? What would be the point of confronting her with proof that this person used to exist?

Moreover, Laura seems just as uninterested as Naomi in bringing Naomi into her previous life, or even speaking to her about it.

When Naomi comes home at night, Laura stands up from the chair and kisses her on the mouth. The lipstick leaves a faint mark.

Naomi puts on a CD.

They have a glass of wine together.

Naomi shares anecdotes from her workday, and Laura laughs. Laura asks lots of questions. She wants to know everyone's names, what they look like, all the details from Naomi's day, and for the first time in a very long while, Naomi feels interested in herself.

In many ways it's an idyllic existence.

At least Naomi has not been this happy in many years.

For the first time in a very long while she's got the sense that what is happening to her is happening because it's meant to be. She's got a sense that someone is watching over her. She's got a sense that life has begun, that the curtain has come up. The life she lived before—it wasn't a bad life. She got up in the morning, she went to the radio house, she did everything she was supposed to do. She didn't lack friends. She didn't lack habits or things that made her happy. But it wasn't a remarkable existence in any way.

On her way home from the radio house she passes the Chinese restaurant and decides to get food for take-out.

She's done this many times before. She's sitting at the bar with her chin in her hand while she waits for her and Laura's dinner. She's waited like this more times than she can count, waited for dinner to take home and eat in front of the TV. It's strange, she thinks, but I never felt back then that life lacked meaning. There was another life, yet another life, before that, too, but it's almost impossible to recall, it feels like fiction, far too distant. Now, the thought of her former self is almost surreal: the thought that she's been sitting with her chin in her hand, staring off into space, in the exact same place where she's sitting now. There was meaning to spare back then, and yet now, afterward, it feels as if life has only recently become real. Yes. She is given the white plastic bag with the warm take-out containers. She pays and receives her change. Steam blooms from the plastic bag when she exits into the chilly air. The inside of the bag fogs up.

When she unlocks the door, Laura stands from the chair and kisses her on the mouth.

They eat in the kitchen.

At night she says, We're no longer strangers.

Laura's pupils are big in the darkness. Naomi has fetched a big glass of water they both drink from. No, Laura says, we really aren't strangers anymore.

So what are we, then? Naomi asks.

Do we have to call each other something? Laura says. Isn't it enough that we're not strangers?

Naomi turns around. She's spilled a bit of water on her pillow and now she puts her cheek on the wet stain. Yes, she says, maybe that's enough. Laura turns around, and Naomi hears how she puts the empty water glass on the floor.

At night, another night, Naomi whispers into Laura's neck.

Do you think we have the same soul? Do you think we're made of the same matter? It's not impossible. We could have been the same person in a previous life. We could be made of the same matter. What if our souls melded, what if we could exist in the same body? Do you think we once did? Do you think you could turn into me?

Laura turns around and strokes her hair, but says nothing.

At night, another night, Naomi braids her fingers into Laura's and whispers, I noticed it on the way down, that something was wrong, but I could have noticed much later, if I hadn't slipped my hands into my pockets, if I hadn't wanted to put my gloves on, if I'd been distracted that day. I could have gotten farther, I could have gotten all the way home, and then I might never have found you again. How incredible that I took your coat, that I changed my life by doing that, all without knowing, and what if I'd never done it—no, I don't even want to have that thought. Just think, you were right the first time you saw me, just think that you knew already then. That I would become your new life. Imagine if I'd known.

Naomi loves to trace their story back, follow this brief tale, picture them sitting at that café table. In their history, one night is still forever. She loves to divulge her feelings. It's not without risk, but also not without pleasure.

In the morning, over the open newspaper, the coffee

cups, the oranges and the eggshells, she watches Laura. In the daytime, when she's at the radio house, she fantasizes about what Laura is doing at home while she waits. Is she watching TV? Is she listening to music? Is she looking out the window, at the naked tree in the yard? Does she go for a little walk?

Every night Naomi falls asleep before Laura, and Laura is alone for a while. If sleep doesn't come she sometimes gets up, fills the water glass in the kitchen, sets it on the counter, half full, and goes to the leather armchair in the living room, where she usually sits in the daytime. She puts her hands in her lap and looks at the shadows and the darkness. She listens to the silence.

She returns to bed before Naomi wakes up so Naomi doesn't get worried—so that Naomi, when she does wake up, can look at Laura with her blond hair fanned out over the pillow, with her eyelids closed over pale eyes. Laura doesn't know it, but Naomi can easily tell from her face when she's truly asleep and when she's just pretending to sleep. When she pretends to sleep she looks peaceful, and her face is beautiful, plump. But when she's truly asleep her face is sunken, the corners of her mouth strive downward, and her cheeks and eyelids are slack, like a corpse.

Before long, spring has arrived. It rains heavily at night and the daytime air is cold and damp. This is just awful, Felix says, today is awful, the kind of cold that gets to your bones. I haven't forgotten the book by the way, I'm going to give it to you, remind me later and I'll give it to you. I feel kind of hoarse today. Naomi, don't you think I sound kind of hoarse? I think I sound kind of creaky, I need to drink some water. I'll just make my voice deeper, it's going to be a seductive baritone kind of day.

At night they watch a TV movie. It's an old film. A thriller.

I love her, Laura whispers. That actress, I recognize her.

The film ends with a murder. It's an ending that's open to interpretation.

At night Laura can't sleep, and once Naomi has fallen asleep Laura gets up, fills the water glass in the kitchen, sets it on the floor beside the leather armchair in the living room, and sits down. Now and then she drinks from the glass. She looks at the shadows and the darkness, she listens to the silence.

Over the weekend they go to Rigardi for a coffee. Cars drive past outside the vaulted windows. In the mirror behind the bar Laura keeps an eye on the door, which keeps opening and closing.

It begins to rain on their walk home. It's a wild, intense rain, with big, fat raindrops. Water rushes, frothing, over the asphalt. They hold each other's hands, they scramble down the sidewalk, they're soaked in a minute, and once they get inside they run up the stairs before they stop on the landing, out of breath.

They take a shower. Naomi puts out her arm, then she takes Laura's arm and straightens it next to her own. Look, it's almost impossible to tell who's who.

Naomi puts the kettle on, then the radio; they drink a

cup of tea, they eat bread with honey, they listen to the rain hitting the windowpanes. I love this sound, Naomi says.

It rains all day. At night it stops. One single, stubborn drip continues. The sound keeps Laura awake. She gets up and moves to the leather armchair. After some time she returns to bed, and when Naomi wakes up a few hours later, when the alarm clock rings, she sees Laura with her blond hair fanned out across the pillow, her cheeks full and rosy, her eyes closed. She puts on coffee, she makes two eggs. She takes the metro to the radio house. She sits down on the train. She reads CITY.

Life is, in most aspects, the same, she thinks to herself. She goes through the same motions as before she met Laura, she sees the same people. Anne gives her a mint candy; she puts it in her pocket. She goes home. She stands on board the train.

What sets life before apart from life after, Naomi thinks, is that somebody is waiting for her. She likes the thought that somebody is thinking about her in the daytime. She also likes the thought that nobody knows— that nobody can tell from looking at her how her life has changed. In many ways life is the same, yes, though she doesn't go to the pool anymore, nor to the department store café, and she barely sees her friends. She wants to spend as much time as possible with Laura. When she comes home, Laura stands up from the armchair and kisses her on the mouth, and the next day the exact same thing repeats.

In this way the weeks go by, and then a month.

Only sometimes does she feel sad that she doesn't

know more about Laura, that Laura hasn't told her more things, that Laura is so quiet. Only sometimes is she frightened by the thought that her conviction that they in some inexplicable way belong together, that they have the same soul, that they could be transformed into each other, that they could meld, that there is nothing that separates them, is necessary since she in fact knows very little about Laura, since Laura, in many respects, remains a stranger to her. Only sometimes is she frightened by the thought that her conviction might be based solely on this lack of intimacy; that she, perhaps, needs the conviction of a supernatural intimacy to compensate. She's frightened to think what Laura is not telling her, and what might be concealed in what Laura is not revealing, for instance, a desire for something other than their calm, quiet, and gentle routines.

In the daytime, when Naomi has left the house, it sometimes happens that Laura goes to lie down on Naomi's side of the bed, which is still a bit warm. It sometimes happens that she falls asleep there again and sleeps until late in the afternoon.

Often, she watches TV.

Often, she stands in front of Naomi's fridge and looks at a postcard that's put up with a magnet. The magnet isn't decorated at all, it's entirely neutral, functional, just a black, matte circle, but the postcard depicts a cadaver, an oil painting of a cadaver. A slaughtered ox. She stands there for a long time and looks at one of the color fields in the painting, a field of black and red.

Naomi comes home. She puts on a CD. A record with duduk music.

What's this? Laura says. Is that a human voice? No, Naomi says, it's a wind instrument. I could have sworn it was a human voice, Laura says. They listen to the music, which billows out into the room like smoke. Yes, Naomi says, I see what you mean.

They have a glass of wine together.

I feel like a ghost, Laura says.

Naomi is silent. She doesn't want to hear what Laura is saying.

I'm bored in the daytime, Laura clarifies.

I understand, Naomi says, quietly.

It hurts her feelings to hear that Laura is bored, but she can't blame her. It hurts her feelings that it's not enough for Laura that she comes home at night, that longing for her isn't enough for the daytime. But she can't blame her.

They go to bed. Naomi falls asleep. Laura is awake. She gets up and sits down in the leather armchair. She looks at the door, the dark hall, she looks at everything that materializes when her eyes get used to the dark: the spines of the books in the bookcases, the doorknob that gleams, and the skinny woman stepping out of the shadows. She listens to the silence, to the little sounds. She returns to bed.

When she wakes up, after turning off the alarm clock, Naomi sits for a long while and looks at Laura's blond, fanned-out hair.

She stands up on the train. For a moment she's got the sense that somebody is staring at her, but when she turns around she sees nothing out of the ordinary.

I GO TO SUBMONDO TO WATCH A MOVIE. SUBMONDO IS located in a basement with a door that tends to jam. The film has already started when I get there, but it doesn't matter. Submondo lets you come and go as you please. It's still light out when I get there, but inside the theater it's dark, lights off. I take a seat in the far back and sink into the soft red velvet.

Today's screening is a movie about a woman who becomes witness to a murder.

She sees it all in a mirror.

Over and over, we're shown what the woman witnessed in the mirror. An image of a shiny knife being raised. An image of the mirror that's suddenly splattered with blood.

Watching the movie, I can't stop thinking about the woman's nails. They're perfectly oval, painted in mother-of-pearl white. I watch the woman's nails as she holds a white Bakelite phone receiver, as she lights a cigarette, as she opens her marbled green compact to check in the little round makeup mirror that nobody has followed her onto the street, and as she, in one of the film's last scenes, closes her hand around a small silver gun. The gun looks like a toy. She follows the murderer onto the street. She follows the sound of the murderer's footsteps. It's a long take. All you hear is the sound of heels against the sidewalk, like a ricocheting heartbeat. She turns the corner and fires. She shoots the murderer.

But nobody believes her when she says the person she's killed is a murderer. Nobody has heard about the murder she describes, the murder she witnessed, the murder in the mirror. The victim is not missed by anyone. Nobody knows what she's talking about when she tells them what she's seen. They think she's crazy. She's detained and locked up in a mental hospital.

In her iris, in the eye's mirror, we see the murderer's silhouette.

That's the film's final image.

The lights in the theater come on. It's an entertaining movie. The ending is open to interpretation.

When I enter the street again it's dark outside. I walk home along the canal. I unlock the door to my building, cross the yard, and walk up the stairs, all five flights of stairs. I unlock my door and drop the keys in the bowl. I turn on the lights in the hall. I take off my shoes and my coat. I linger in the hall and listen for a moment. I listen to the silence. There are many little sounds in the silence. The sounds of my fridge. The sound of water in the pipes, the sound of the radiators. There are many little sounds I never think about. I'd go crazy if I thought about them all the time.

I brush my teeth. I look at my own reflection while I do it. I'm bored. Toothbrushing is boring and monotonous.

I wash my face, I rub my face with my fingers, and as I rub my face with my fingers something happens that I can't explain. For a moment my skin seems porous. It gives under my fingers, the tips of my fingers sink in as if my face were made of mud, of sand and water. I lift my face from the sink.

I look at my own reflection. I touch my face again. It's wet, but it looks normal, it feels normal. I look around me. I am alone.

It was just a sensation, I tell myself. Just a feeling. It was no more than a feeling—no less, but no more, either. I dry my face with the scratchy towel and my face holds, it has no give. I brush my hair, I pull hard with the brush, I tear it across my scalp and my scalp doesn't move, and my hair doesn't come off my head.

I go to bed, and I lie there in the dark and listen to the silence, and I think, I'm alone.

I was the eldest of five siblings, the others were all boys, and every summer we'd take a photo where our parents arranged us according to height: first me and then my brothers, one, two, three, four, like a ladder. Then, one summer, my brother closest to me in age had passed me in height, so we switched places. The following summer all my brothers had started to grow past each other this way and that, we were arranged all pell-mell in the picture. My second brother was the tallest, and every one except for our youngest brother had grown past me. He was always my favorite. Finally he, too, grew past me, leaving me the shortest of the bunch, and that summer I realized that we had become adults. From the first picture to the last I had moved from left to right. We never took a photo like that again, but I've kept them in an album...

In the summer, the summer before I got married, I went on a bicycle vacation... We biked to the ocean. We biked a whole week. It was me and my closest girlfriends. One of them had brought a camera. I never saw the pictures she took... oh, how I would like to see those pictures ... we fell out of touch ... and now she's dead ... but enough about her. This is supposed to be about me. At that time I was young. Back then biking to the ocean was enough. Such simple pleasures. Back then, that was the most fun you could imagine. Later on, it was other things ... yes ... later on, diversions were more complex ... more complex and more expensive. That summer, when we biked to the sea, we brought a tent. But sometimes we slept under the sky—often, we did. Did we ever sleep in that tent? Did we need to? Now I can't remember anymore. Though I do remember the way we struggled to put it up, so at some point we must have ... unless it was just to test how ... it was a blue, a blue tent, and it smelled of, well, tent ... We'd brought food, bread, and jam, and coffee that we'd make. So we had ... we lived off bread and a jar of jam all week ... how slender we were ... no need for anything else ... and the coffee ... And the highlight of the entire trip was going to be the ocean, and it was lovely, yes, it was. I remember spotting it from afar. A flat landscape. The sea was glittering in the distance ... we biked ... there ... and tossed our bikes ... and jumped in ... it was cliffs, pink cliffs, and of course, salty water the likes of which I'd never seen in my life ... and chilly, chilly! At the time I thought salt water was special ... this was one of my life's highlights ... we lay there and dried off in the sun for a moment. And then we biked back. That was it. That was the whole of it. Of course we must have been tired when we got to the sea, and even worse on the way home when we'd biked for several days ... and on those old, stiff bikes with hard saddles ... though they work well, those bikes ... better than new bicycles ... Today I don't remember any such feelings, no fatigue at all. The sea ... yes, it was pretty. But my favorite aspect, that was lying there at night before we fell asleep and just ... yes ... lying down under the night sky next to my best friend ... before life had truly started ... and to feel so alive ...

When I woke up in my bedroom I had a view of the garden, a big oak tree atop the hill leading to the house next door, and how green it was, our garden ... a veritable jungle ... so green you couldn't even see the house next door, though you knew it was there ... It was a real dream, that garden ... true paradise ... with laburnum bushes, rhododendron ... there were cherry trees ... big, black cherries ... and apricots, peaches ... peaches all along the wall up to my bedroom window. They're such pretty trees, with pink blossoms. In August all I had to do was open the window and put my hand out to pluck a fruit. August was always my favorite month. Because of this, because of the peaches... It's been a long time since I ate a peach this way. Lots of people don't know that peaches are very—when you pluck them like this, that they're very downy... not like in the stores... not just a bit... how can I put this... the peaches in the store, it's as if somebody had shaved them, they're smooth like suede. But a peach, a peach like that, the peaches I ate as a child, the ones I plucked from my window, they were furry all over. My entire mouth would fill with down when I took a bite. It's how I wanted it. If I could eat a peach like that again... I would be so happy... Next I'll attempt to describe my room, best as I can. Details. The walls were pale blue with daisies, it could have been a wallpaper or perhaps they were painted onto the wall—I'm realizing, in fact, that I'm not sure, and there's no way for me to check... I've got this photograph... but I don't think it would be possible to say just from looking at it... no, I'll give you artistic license here, it doesn't matter to me if you write that it was wallpaper or paint...

And every night, throughout my childhood, I would clasp my hands over my chest and pray to God that He would let me grow up fast. I was terribly afraid of the dark, so the door to my bedroom was always cracked open at night, and the image of that yellow crack, and the sound of my parents' and sometimes their guests' voices there down the hallway, that sound is forever associated with prayer for me...Please, Lord...let me grow up fast...let me...leave this place...When I close my eyes I still hear those sounds and see that image... the yellow crack...the door cracked open... it's as if I were still there...that image never goes away...and I wonder...I have to ask... where time really went...

I GET TO WORK. I LISTEN. I LISTEN DILIGENTLY ALL WEEK. I diligently write down everything I hear, every word, every silence, every sigh.

When I go out at night, when I go out for groceries, when I go out for a little glass of wine at Rigardi, when I go out for a walk by the canal in order to mark the end of the workday and the beginning of my free time, I check my pocket for the transcription. When I come through the door, I take off my shoes and unfold the piece of paper.

I have seen you. Have you seen me?

When I go to bed I lie there and listen to the silence. I listen to the little sounds. The sound of my fridge and the sound of my radiators.

One day it rains, and the storm almost drowns out the sound of the recordings as I work. It crashes against the window, it crashes down the drainpipes, it batters and clatters against the world outside my kitchen. I hammer on the keys to keep myself from being distracted by the rain.

I wash my face before I go to bed and it happens again: my face gives, it sinks at my fingertips, like mud. This time the sensation lingers. It doesn't go away. Standing in front of the mirror, I touch my face with my fingers, and I see with my own eyes the way the fingers sink in. I blink. My face is porous, it doesn't hold.

I tell myself that I have to avoid touching it. I need to let it be.

The ghostwriter and I eat dinner at an Italian restaurant. The restaurant has checkered tablecloths, wax candles in wine bottles, plastic grapes that look perfectly real. I squeeze one of them. The leaves give them away, the leaves are obviously made from cloth, with plastic veins on the back. The ghostwriter looks at the cluster of grapes, then at me. They look perfectly real, he says, and he opens the menu.

He orders sparkling water and wine, a bottle of wine. Red. The wine comes fast, the bottle is wrapped in straw, the glasses are round and small. They give us bread, and olive oil in a glass bottle. I pour some oil on my plate and salt it. I press the bread against the plate, then I eat it.

The ghostwriter is paying.

The ghostwriter and I drink a little glass of wine before the food arrives. The ghostwriter orders for us. We are having the same thing. Spaghetti with tomato sauce. The plates are steaming when the waiter sets them on the table, and we're given a small bowl of grainy, pale cheese, and a small spoon to take the cheese with. This, the ghostwriter says, letting the cheese rain over the spaghetti, doesn't have much in common with real parmesan. But it's tasty!

Italian songs play on the speakers. The volume is loud. I drink the wine. I eat the food.

Did you hear the rain the other day? the ghostwriter asks. Yes, I say. I love that sound, he says. It's rare for it to rain this time of year. Usually it's too cold for rain.

The ghostwriter puts down his silverware and picks up his napkin, dabbing at the corners of his mouth. He folds the napkin into a little triangle before doing so. The napkin is burgundy red, textured and thin, and once he's finished dabbing the corner of his mouth he folds it into an even smaller triangle.

You look kind of pale, he says. Not a lot of color on you.

I put down my silverware. The bubbles in my water are reflected in the blade of the knife. I look at the reflection of the bubbles, then I look at the ghostwriter.

Have you ever heard something that scared you? I ask him.

He places the folded napkin on the checkered tablecloth. The little triangle opens. The ghostwriter folds it again and shoves it under his plate. He shakes his head.

No, he says. Nothing scares me.

Nothing? I say.

Nothing, the ghostwriter says.

He pulls a toothpick from a little wooden container and pushes it out of the white wrapper.

Sometimes, he continues. Some people...they've experienced such...

Yes, I say.

He digs in his mouth with the toothpick.

But they're rare, he says. No, I can't say I've ever heard anything that scared me.

He keeps digging.

Life is over in a minute, he says. Yes, I say.

At some point there will be nobody alive who knows we existed, he says. Have you ever thought about that? Yes, I say.

Art is man's only chance at an eternal life, he says and smacks his lips. Yes, I say.

Do you want dessert? he asks.

The ghostwriter loves food. He orders single espressos and tiramisu. He orders for both of us.

It's just me, the ghostwriter, and the women themselves who know the breadth of the stories of their lives. Only we know what they say when they're alone. When they're instructed to tell everything. With as much detail and truthfulness as possible. Only we know what they share before saying, Don't include this. There is an instruction in the manual that reads: If something is difficult to share, you can share it several times, so that it eventually turns into a story, something that didn't happen to you. Record it all, all the versions. You can start over as many times as you'd like. It's fine if it's incoherent. I'll take care of that later.

They tell their stories, again and again. I listen. I'm prepared for most things. I don't judge, nor does the ghostwriter. We don't judge anyone. I just write what they say, word for word. My hands are the tools of my trade, not my heart. Not my head.

No fate has ever scared me. None of the terrible things I've heard have scared me. No description of what other people have done to the women. I have heard a woman describe, in great detail, what she did over the course of several days to poison her husband, and the effects of the poison on his body.

Sometimes it is unpleasant to hear, sure. Uncomfortable. But it's not frightening.

The only thing that's ever frightened me is the whispering voice.

We drink our coffees and eat our desserts. The music is loud from the speakers, it seems as if they turn up the volume a little bit every minute. Wax drips from the candle in the wine bottle and onto the checkered cloth. The Italian restaurant is warm and comfortable. I'm drowsy from the warmth and the wine, full and sleepy. I clasp my hands on the table and look at my dry knuckles.

Something strange happened to me recently, I say.

Something strange? the ghostwriter asks and licks the dessert spoon.

Something strange, I repeat. Something that frightened me.

The ghostwriter puts down the spoon. His knuckles, I now discover, are also dry. He looks at me with a concerned expression. He's ready to listen.

I falter. I search for a way to tell him, but I can't find the words. I can't find the words to explain why the recording I heard, the voice I heard, frightened me. I can't find the words to explain to him that I have recently felt increasingly diffuse, as if I were disappearing. I would like to ask him to touch my face, but I can't bring myself to do it. I wish I could ask him to affirm me.

We sit across from each other in silence, our hands clasped. When I look at my own hands, the skin is almost transparent. The bones are white underneath. The nails are thin.

Most things in this world have a logical explanation,

the ghostwriter says. I still haven't said anything. He picks up his spoon again and begins to scrape the edges of his plate. Usually the things that frighten us are completely innocuous, or not even real. The imagination can run wild at night.

Yes, I say. Yes.

I look at my hands, and for an instant I can see straight through them. Yes: my hands are no more than a set of diffuse contours. Looking through them I see the checkered tablecloth, the little coffee cups, the plates, the wooden toothpick holder.

I blink and look at the ghostwriter again. My hands return.

What do you think, the ghostwriter says, shall we? Tomorrow is another day.

It's true. Tomorrow is another day. And we've got lots of work right now. Lots of people who are getting in touch.

The ghostwriter asks for the check and pays. He helps me with my coat, then puts on his own. We enter the street and the darkness.

It's cold, the ghostwriter says. Must be below freezing. Do you feel that? It smells like fire.

Yes, I say, it's true. It does smell like fire.

We walk into the metro together, BANG. Yellow tile on the walls.

Urine yellow, the ghostwriter says.

He looks around. He looks delighted. I wonder if he's going to use that in any of the books. Urine yellow.

The ghostwriter's train arrives first. He squeezes my hand before he embarks and leaves me alone.

Sometimes I think that my job is more honest than the ghostwriter's. My job is to listen and write. I don't make anything up. I don't add anything. I just write down what the women say. The ghostwriter's job is to bring order to the women's lives. His work is to find the story. He finds the drama. He crosses out the women's own literary turns of phrase and adds his own. The ghostwriter takes pride in having no presence in the red book; his own name is nowhere. But he does have a style. I don't know if he understands it himself, but he really does have a style. It's distinctive. I would only need to read a few sentences to recognize a text as his.

With my work it's different. I leave no trace. I am just there to listen. I am just there to write what I hear.

If my hands began to give, I wouldn't be able to work.

I don't know what I'd do in that situation.

I would need to do something different with my life.

I know there was a life when I didn't work for the ghostwriter, but I can no longer remember it. I don't remember what I did then. I don't remember how I lived. All I know is traveling to the ghostwriter's office, once at the start of the week and once at the end of the week, and in between, listening. Listening and typing.

I no longer remember when I began working for the ghostwriter. It feels as if it was very recently, and also as if it was a long time ago.

I'm afraid of disappearing.

I'm afraid of what that would entail.

Late in life I learned that I had a sister. Late, late, after my husband died, as well as my eldest son... I already mentioned... my siblings were dead, and my parents of course, and I was so lonely in that big house, this house where I'd lived almost all my life. I didn't think there was anyone in the whole world who knew, nobody alive, no relative—my younger son, sure, and my grandchildren, but nobody who—nobody who had ... maybe ... nobody who had memories of me as a child, or memories of our parents, and who just ... yes ... nobody who'd lived in that world, which I thought I was completely alone with. Then one day, entirely out of the blue, there was a letter: Hello, I am so-and-so, and... she had... she had, this was a biological sister, we had the same parents, she wrote our parents' names... and my name... my former name. To think that I'd had a sister! My whole life! A sister! A full sister—that's what she wrote. Yes... a full sister who had lived with me for some time. Who lived with me a long time ago. She wanted to meet me, of course. She had ... I don't think ... I don't think she'd had a very pleasant life... That's the sense I got... but the thing is, she'd known about me for all these years, all these years she'd known I existed, and she hadn't attempted—at least she didn't mention it in the letter. No. Well, of course I can't know for sure . . . Maybe—maybe she'd been looking for me . . . and hadn't found me until then. Who knows. Who knows. She was, let's see, she was seven years older than me. Seven, she was seven when I was born. So you can imagine—she was as old as the hills. And she didn't want . . . but I couldn't! I just couldn't do it! No! It was as if the whole world had collapsed . . . like an earthquake . . . I just cried and cried . . . and I thought about the world we'd lived in, which will never be again . . . and here I'd been thinking it was completely . . . lost . . . I'd been thinking that I was absolutely, completely alone with it . . . and I couldn't bear it . . . no . . . I couldn't bear it . . . to see her . . . to hear her speak . . . to see her . . . I was afraid . . . afraid of what could . . .

It was never my wish to move. Oh no, I don't like cities, I never liked it here. I can say that now. I have never liked it here. And I don't think I ever will. It is what it is. I dislike the landscape. My husband would always say, But why don't we get in the car, we can drive out to the forest, into nature. But it's the wrong kind of nature! The nature here, I never liked it. It's the wrong kind of trees . . . not like the ones we had back home ... what I think of as home ... and the wrong kind of light. I've never managed to explain it to anyone, explain what I mean when I say it's the wrong kind of light ... this light is shiny and slick, like on a stage set. My husband took me out into nature, he'd drive us in the car, and we walked around in that forest ... in these terrible forests ... with that awful, awful light ... And I pretended to be happy and grateful. And of course it was ... yes ... he loved me a lot, taking me on those excursions that had no value for him. You know, he was from the city. He liked cities. Though actually, now that I think of it, he really enjoyed driving, so I'm sure he got something out of those outings, after all. The journey itself. To drive out of ... and to drive fast! Yes, I think so ... I think he liked it ... so in his world there was something for both of us in those countryside outings. I got to be in nature, and he got to drive. But I've never gotten over ... I've never been able to love that kind of nature ... not like I loved nature back home. It's not even—I mean, I'm not a biologist, I'm not a birder ... I know nothing about herbs and that sort of thing ... it doesn't interest me. I've got a hard time remembering things. Names. I've got no interest whatsoever in categorizing. It would probably have been easier if I did. I imagine that would make it lovely to arrive in a new place, with a different sort of nature, but I don't find it interesting at all. No. No ... nature ... it's all sentimental to me ... just entirely ... emotional ...

I don't know how to talk about this, or where to put it in my life—I suppose that will be your job, later—but I'd like to say something about the happy moments. I mean the simple, happy moments. They are many, after all. I'd like to preserve them somehow. I want to keep them. Yes. In print. I want this to be written down, so that someone in the future could point to it and say, She was happy, she was often happy. But it's difficult—it's difficult to choose one specific memory. Perhaps it should be something where, maybe something where there are several memories combined into one, one single scene. Because I have such a ... I've got these memories of happiness. And if it's one single— one single memory. What could it be? Well ... let me think. I know, I should include details ... we could do ... yes, I remember ... this dinner party, a party on Epiphany Eve, we were melting tin to predict the future, and it was—well, what would we have eaten, seafood? And I'd guess there were at least twenty of us around the big table, and all the children ... that's a happy memory. Walking through the park in the fall. The thought of walking through the park in the fall ... sometimes the thought of it beats the actual walk. But to wake up one day, on a fall day, and think, Today I'm going to take a walk through the park. That's a happy memory. What I'm getting at here—what I'm trying to capture ... it's the little things. The simple things ... and ... yes, this one, too: to wake up and stay in bed ...

It's difficult to know what impact you have on other people. In your lifetime. Sitting here talking like this, I think about all the people who've touched my life and they didn't even know it at all. And everyone whose life I've touched without realizing. Everyone and everything ... it sounds as if I ... well ... it sounds boastful ... that's not how I mean it ... but perhaps that's still something I can let myself hope. That there's somebody out there ... somebody that I, how can I put it, that I've touched in some way ...

Let's see here: The day we moved in, what do I recall from that day? Was it sunny, was it ... For some reason I know it was a Sunday, I remember that much, that it was Sunday—for some reason that's stuck with me! Sunday ... Sunday ... yes ... A word I always liked ... really, what a funny word ... but I'm rambling!

NAOMI IS TRYING TO PUT ON A NECKLACE IN FRONT OF the mirror. This is the worst, she mumbles. She sees her hands, sees the necklace—the thin silver chain—and the clasp of the necklace, the two parts that need to join, and she sees the fingers that are holding the clasp, the fingers that look enormous in comparison. There's a drip from the bathtub faucet. The stopper hangs from its chain, which is wrapped around the tap to keep it from slipping. It's an enervating sound. She tries again and again. She needs to look in the mirror to see what she's doing but she needs to do the opposite, the opposite of what looks logical. Instead of closing the necklace she moves the two parts away from each other.

Here, let me, Laura says, and she closes the necklace without difficulty. She adjusts the thin chain. She caresses Naomi's neck with her big hands. Naomi looks at the two of them in the bathroom cabinet mirror, its rounded edges framing them, and she sees that the mirror is a little spotted, sees fingerprints where they have opened and closed the cabinet, sees her own face, familiar, the way she always sees herself, and she sees Laura's face, a little strange, a little asymmetrical. Her blond hair is unwashed. Her face is sallow.

Naomi leaves the apartment, shutting the door behind her.

A short while later, Laura, too, leaves the home. She's

wearing Naomi's button-down, Naomi's skirt, Naomi's tights, and Naomi's loafers, which are a bit too small.

She goes to the supermarket. This chain looks the same everywhere. The same logo, the same jingle playing from the speakers, the same voice announcing sales prices. She's not been to the supermarket in a while. Not in a long while. She picks up a basket and slowly walks through the store. She puts a bunch of grapes in the basket. She walks past the bread, the meat, the fish, the shelves with flour and coffee, detergent, cheap toys, candy, alcohol. It's not crowded. She's in no rush. Finally she goes to the aisle with hygiene and beauty products, pink hairspray cans, wax, acetone, Q-tips, and the shelves stocked with hair dye. She looks at the models who smile with their big mouths and voluminous manes of hair. She holds up one of the boxes and closes her eyes, picturing Naomi's head and her dark, almost black hair, the way it looks against the white pillow in the morning and at night, what it's like to run her hand through Naomi's hair when it's newly washed and wet, or dry and soft, or shiny with hair oil—though Naomi doesn't like anyone to touch her hair then—and she opens her eyes again, comparing Naomi with the woman on the box. She puts it back.

How would she describe Naomi's hair color if she had to use a single word? *Ebony* is the first that comes to mind, but there's no visual when she tries it. It's a word she's heard somewhere.

After careful consideration, after comparing the different boxes with dark-brown hair dye, she finally selects one. It's sink or swim.

She limps as she walks back home, and once she gets inside and takes off Naomi's loafers she discovers that the shoes have chafed her so badly that the tights are sticking to her blood and pus. The insoles are stained. She tries to clean them with a cotton round, but the leather inside the shoes is blond and the blood is dark. She puts them away in the closet.

Next she rinses the grapes, puts them in a bowl, and sets the bowl on the kitchen table. She combs her hair with water in the bathroom, tucks it behind her ears, and cuts it right at the earlobe. She flushes the blond tufts down the drain. The pipes gurgle. She wraps her shoulders with a pale-yellow towel and dyes her hair. The dye is perfumed. It reeks of fruit. What fruit, Laura can't say. This fruit perfume isn't quite able to conceal the dye's sharp, chemical scent.

She rinses her hair. She combs it with oil. She reads the oil's list of ingredients. *Prunus armeniaca.*

She looks at herself in the mirror and immediately realizes that the results are not quite what she'd hoped for. She had imagined they would look more alike. But from far away, or from behind—yes, it's not impossible. Not unthinkable. Someone who doesn't know Naomi might very well confuse Laura for her. Still, it's not what she'd expected.

She spends the rest of the day waiting for Naomi, fantasizing about her reaction.

Naomi is frightened when she comes home in the evening, but she does her best to hide it. It's clear that Laura needs affirmation. Laura kisses Naomi on the mouth. Her neck is a little stained by the dye, which is much too reddish, and her hair is choppy.

Did you do it so you'd look like me? Naomi asks, though the answer is obvious.

Laura nods. I thought you'd like it, she says. What do you think?

Naomi grieves Laura's previous look, her blond hair and the way it appeared on the pillow when she woke up, but says nothing.

The next morning Naomi leaves to go to the radio house, and Laura drinks a cup of coffee in the kitchen. She touches her hair, unaccustomed to feel it end at the ears, and listens to the radio. Felix is on in the mornings, Anne in the afternoons, but the sound technician is the same throughout the day.

She puts on Naomi's clothes and Naomi's perfume and goes out for a little walk.

When Naomi gets home that evening she runs into one of her neighbors in the stairwell. I saw you earlier, he says, I tried to say hi but it seemed like you didn't hear me, you were on your way out, you seemed like you were in a rush. Yes, Naomi says. Yes. I guess I didn't see you. I guess I didn't hear you. I'm always lost in thought in the mornings. No, the neighbor says, it wasn't in the morning, it was just a few hours ago. It can't have been me, then, Naomi says. I was at work. That explains it, the neighbor says, that makes sense that I didn't get an answer when I said your name.

She walks up the stairs and unlocks the door and Laura stands up from the leather armchair. She's wearing Naomi's bathrobe and her hair is wet and shiny. Did you go outside today? Naomi asks. No, says Laura.

Naomi puts on a CD and pours a glass of wine. She sees that Laura has been eating grapes. Their skeleton is in the sink.

They go to bed. They fall asleep at about the same time.

When Naomi wakes up in the morning and turns off the alarm she sits up in bed and looks for a while at Laura's dark head against the pillow, her closed eyes, her hairline, still a little blotchy from the dye. It's going to fade, she thinks. Hair grows. But she still can't chase the grief she feels at this sight, the badly dyed hair. She gets up and makes coffee, she boils two eggs, she throws out the empty egg carton, she puts on the radio. It's the requests show. Someone has asked for *Dance of the Blessed Spirits*. Felix plays it and when the music ends the news starts.

Laura enters the kitchen when the news broadcast is over. Naomi has opened the newspaper over the kitchen table. Laura peels an egg and looks out the window. She drinks her coffee. She peels an orange and eats it. She puts the orange peel in her empty coffee cup. She listens to the radio. Naomi combs her hair in the bathroom, applies oil, gets dressed, drinks a glass of tap water in the kitchen, kisses Laura's forehead and strokes her cheek.

She takes the metro to the radio house and looks out the window as the train travels aboveground, looks at the buildings and the platforms, the sky and the cautious trees, the rain that hammers violently against the scratched windowpane, at her own pale cheek.

Laura takes Naomi's mother-of-pearl nail polish from

the bathroom cabinet and sits down in the kitchen. The sun is shining through the window. She spreads her fingers. She paints her nails. But the varnish floats out and pools in her cuticles, which are yellow from peeling the orange, and when she cautiously checks to see if it's dried she presses too hard. Looking at her nails, her ugly, ruined nails, she feels despair.

She throws out the eggshells and the orange peels, washes the coffee cups and plates, folds the paper. She combs and applies oil to her hair, but she still can't quite get it to lay like she wants it to. She gets dressed, pulling in her stomach to be able to button the pants. She smells of anxious sweat. She puts on perfume. Her fingers are still yellow from the orange, even though she's washed her hands. She looks at herself in the mirror and tries to take deep, calm breaths. She's as unaccustomed to her new look as Naomi is. The dark hair, she feels, looks odd with her pale eyebrows.

She gets Naomi's loafers from the closet and goes outside. Walking hurts, but she's going to have to get used to it. She walks past the square and the market with vegetables and honey jars and coats and leather jackets hanging from their rods, tables with pots and china and toys. She enters the metro and stamps her ticket. It's sucked into the machine and spat out again, BANG. She finds a seat on the train. She leans her forehead against the scratched windowpane. She's not on her way anywhere. She wants to pass the time. She travels without a plan. Once the train reaches its end station, on the outskirts of the city, she stays in her seat with her forehead against the windowpane while the other passengers disembark. The train idles at the station for a few minutes, soon filling up with new passengers. There's an issue of CITY on the seat next to her and she picks it up and puts it in her lap to make space, in case somebody would like to sit next to her, but nobody takes the seat next to her.

She rides to the other end station. The outskirts of cities, she thinks, almost always look identical.

New people get on and off the train.

They move again.

Laura holds on to the issue of CITY without opening the paper. She readies herself to get off the train. Too late. It's only when it leaves the stop with the yellow tiles that she realizes she's gone too far. The next time it stops they're aboveground, an old station, a cast-iron station, and she gets off, leaving the paper on the seat. The air smells of trash and piss and bread. It's crowded around the station. She looks around. Nobody is looking at her, nobody looks at her as if they've seen each other before, nobody appears to recognize her. She runs her hand through her hair and her fingers get oily, she puts her hand in her pocket, rubbing it against the slippery lining, then walks past the photo booth and the phone booth and down the stairs and out onto the street. She tries to find her way home, to Naomi's house, by instinct. She sets off in the direction she thinks is right. Soon the crowds thin. She's alone on the street. There are no cars, and the sounds of the city seem more cushioned, muffled by the buildings around her. Soon all she hears is the sound of her own shoes hitting the ground, like ricocheting heartbeats. She walks past a laundromat, and the air smells sharply of detergent. She pauses and looks at the machines that move with intensity behind the glass, spinning and foaming in a loud struggle, and then she walks past a bakery, the air smelling of warm flour. She looks down the street that continues. She stands there, with the bakery and the laundromat at her back. There's nothing down the street. No store. No person.

She no longer knows where to go, she no longer trusts her instinct.

She returns to the metro to ride to the stop before this one. As she climbs the stairs, a flash goes off in the photo booth, and while she hurries to the train, which is already at the platform, she bumps into someone who comes walking in the opposite direction, nearly losing her balance. She doesn't turn around.

When Naomi comes home, Laura gets up from the leather armchair. Did you go outside today? Did you see anyone? No, Laura says. No.

Laura walks into the living room again and puts on a CD, the one with duduk music. Naomi pours a glass of wine. The phone rings and Naomi goes to pick it up, but before she can get there Laura has the receiver in her hand. Hello, she says, without introducing herself. She locks eyes with Naomi, who is in the doorway with her wineglass. Yes, Laura says. Absolutely. Yes, you, too. Yes, it really was ages ago. Would love to. She tugs at the phone's thick, somewhat grimy corkscrew cord and looks at the ground. Naomi hears Laura do something with her voice. She makes it a little deeper. She clears her throat. The music is hissing out of the CD player.

See you soon, then, she says, and adds, after a moment's hesitation, I'll bring someone, if you don't mind. Yes. Thanks. No, I can't say. Yes, you'll see. You'll see.

She clears her throat again.

Until soon, Laura says.

She hangs up.

Who was that? Naomi asks.

Karl, Laura replies.

Karol, Naomi corrects her.

Karol, she repeats. He invited us over for dinner.

I WALK TO SUBMONDO. I ARRIVE ALONE. I FIND THE CHAIR I want in the red darkness. My eyes slowly acclimatize. I lean back.

They're showing an old film tonight. A thriller.

I read about it in CITY. It's a famous movie. A story of murder, betrayal, and paranoia.

A woman has killed her lover. That's how the film starts.

The murder has already happened when the film begins. I understand that it's already happened. The woman rinses her bloodied hands in a white sink. The blood is bright red, clearly fake. Real blood doesn't look like that. It's not so garish. I don't think so, at least. But in the film's universe it's real.

The woman has blood underneath her nails. She scrubs them clean. I see her hands, the sink, the faucet, and the blood being washed away—only that, not the corpse of her lover, nothing other than her hands and the blood. She's struggling to clean her hands entirely. She labors as the water rushes from the faucet.

As this long film sequence unfolds, the woman washing her hands, I wonder how she did it. What weapon she used. Why she did it.

The woman turns off the faucet and looks at herself in the mirror.

I love this actress. She's beautiful. Her face is soft, her mouth points downward, her eyes are big. I've seen pictures of her in magazines, recent photos, I've seen her middle-aged face, her face as it looks now, different, her mouth that stretches toward the cheeks following a face lift, her tattooed eyebrows, her movie-star hair, which is still very beautiful—thick, dark, and shiny. Maybe she wears a wig. But on the screen in front of me she's still not done anything to her face and her hair is her own, I'm sure of that, this hair that she runs her wet hands through in front of the mirror.

I sink even deeper into my seat.

After she's washed her hands, after she's turned off the faucet and looked at her own reflection, the woman skips town.

She travels to a resort town in the mountains. She finds a hideout in an empty vacation home, a house she doesn't have a key to but whose door is unlocked. The house is modern. A white villa. It's at the top of a hill in a garden. There's a pool that's still got water in it and lots of old leaves. The camera lingers at the unnaturally blue surface of the water and the flat, wet leaves. The house stands out in the landscape, it looks off, oddly modern among the old, rustic homes, old olive trees. Earth and stone. There are no other people nearby. No tourists, no neighbors. It's very quiet. There is a hotel, which the woman can see from her garden, but it's closed for the season. The woman doesn't touch the white sheets that are draped over the house's furniture to protect it from sun. She leaves them in place. She's careful not to touch anything, careful not to leave any trace, she moves in an odd way, effortful, she takes off her shoes, she sleeps without making the bed.

People keep coming and going in the theater. Someone sits down, someone stands up. I'm aware of all the activity, but it doesn't bother me. I'm fully absorbed by the movie.

Eventually, the woman starts to feel as if somebody is hiding from her in the house. She sees shadows. She sees contours, as if of a person, but getting closer it turns out to be an illusion. She thinks she sees something moving under the sheets covering the furniture, but when she pulls them off there's nothing there. At night she hears the sound of footsteps and doors being opened. But perhaps it's all in her imagination. Nobody enters her room. Nobody tears her door open. And in the daytime her fear goes away. In the daytime she's able to distract herself. She swims in the pool despite the dead leaves. She lies down to dry off in the sun. She smokes cigarettes. She drinks coffee.

There's a long, silent scene where she tries to get the espresso machine in the house to work. While this scene unfolds I hear other people in the audience snort in sympathy. Somebody laughs out loud, almost demonstratively.

It's comic relief.

The woman gets increasingly comfortable. She abandons caution. She gets sheets from the linen closet and makes the bed she's been sleeping in. She wears one of the robes from the bathroom. She lets the ashtray overflow, she walks around with her shoes on. She uses the perfume in the bathroom cabinet, she brushes her hair with the owner's hairbrush. She doesn't clean her hair from the brush. She leaves her coffee cups out. She picks up a book and reads it, puts it down somewhere random, picks up another, puts it down.

Were the owners of the house to return, it wouldn't take them long to realize that somebody has moved into their house. They would notice the fragrance of perfume, the scent of old coffee in the trash—perhaps even smell the smell of another person in the sheets. They would see the full ashtray, the coffee cups, the hair in the hairbrush, and the books.

The woman walks to the center of the village, where the permanent residents live. She eats spaghetti at a restaurant. She can't lock the door to the house when she leaves since she doesn't have a key.

After dinner she walks back in the darkness.

The image is pitch-black. You can only sense the woman in the landscape. You hear the sound of her steps on the gravel road. Then she's illuminated by an oncoming bus. She's blinded by the sharp lights and she stumbles and steps to the side, off the road, she holds on to a low stone wall to maintain her balance. The bus passes her and continues down the steep, meandering road. It leaves her in the dark.

At one point in the film there's a continuity error.

I am preoccupied by this error.

In one frame there is violent rain. In the next frame no time has passed, but the rain has stopped and the sun is shining.

The film moves on, but I can't stop thinking about the error. It bothers me. I wonder if it's intentional. I don't understand it. I wonder what it's supposed to mean.

The woman grows paranoid again. She stops leaving the house, she doesn't even go into the garden. She locks all the doors and windows from the inside and she checks again and again to make sure they're truly locked. She listens intently for the sounds again, the sounds of footsteps and doors opening, sounds that are increasingly insistent even in the daytime, and she looks through the glass doors of the summerhouse, looks out at the pool, the hotel that's closed for the season. Her gaze seeks, darts. Her face fills the entire screen, her beautiful, soft face, her big eyes, her full mouth with the worried corners.

In the film's final scene it turns out she's been right. There really is someone hiding from her. Someone hiding in the house.

We never see the stranger's face. Only the stranger's body. The stranger is backlit by the strong sun behind, and the woman inhales sharply. It's not a scream. Just a breath.

The actress has a very beautiful voice. I know this. I've seen her old musical films, I've heard her recordings of famous songs. Her voice is delicate, very unusual. It is bright and breathless. She can't quite sing, she's not a good singer, but her voice is beautiful. She's famous for her voice. She hasn't used it a single time in this film, she's not had a single line—all we hear is her breathing. She's not spoken a word. Just inhaled.

The movie's final frame shows her lifeless body floating in the pool. The ending is open to interpretation.

For the ghostwriter, the ending has always constituted a problem.

He has been commissioned to write a book that

encompasses a whole life, but the women's lives don't end when they purchase the ghostwriter's services.

It's happened that a client has passed away during the course of the work. He's told me this, it's not something I've experienced myself.

When that happens he'll finish the book anyway. He's been paid, after all.

But it's not common. Most of his clients are still alive when he completes their books, and he needs a different kind of ending, an ending that isn't death.

The women's own stories are rarely of any help.

They stop talking when they no longer remember.

They often start out describing their lives in chronological order. They try to do it this way, at first. But they soon lose the thread. Often they'll think of something and promise to return to it later, but forget. Every once in a while the ghostwriter will set up a meeting to ask questions. Or prompt them: You had something important to tell. Something you said you'd get back to.

At that point they often no longer remember what was so important.

No matter what, the ghostwriter would like them to feel pleased with the ending. He wants it to feel satisfying, hopeful, bright, and beautiful; he wants the ending to make life seem big, he wants it to remind them that they've lived, that they've left a mark on the world, that the world is great and the time they spent on Earth is meaningful. That's his wish. Some women, though, ask for a specific ending: spectacular, or sad, or surprising. When that happens he honors their request. He wants them to be happy. That's his highest priority, by far his highest priority. But if he gets to choose, and he often does, he wants the ending to be moving.

Some of the ghostwriter's clients begin, at some point, to speak of their own lives entirely in simple past tense, whether they're talking about the past or not. When I hear them speak about themselves in this way I think to myself that they've already started to imagine themselves as characters in a novel, that they're trying to get ahead of the ghostwriter, that they, on their own, are trying to think of their lives as great, worthy of a story.

I walk home from Submondo. It's cold outside. My hands are cold. I should be wearing gloves. I should be wearing a warmer coat. The coat I have, my trench coat, is actually too light. It's a coat for fall and spring. And this is winter. Winter is already here.

When I get home I drink from a glass I've left standing on the counter. The water smells like rum. I empty the glass and turn on the faucet, but the water won't get cold enough.

I hold the glass in front of me.

My lip hasn't left any mark on the glass, and not my fingers, either. The glass is perfectly clean, as if nobody had touched it. I lick the glass, feeling its cold against my tongue, but my tongue leaves no mark.

I don't understand, but I recall what the ghostwriter told me. Most things in this world have a logical explanation.

I try to look out the window and see only my own reflection. There's nobody there, just me.

I bunch up my fist. My knuckles whiten. I relax again. I spread my fingers. I touch my cheeks. My face is porous but my hands are firm. I can still use my hands.

I put the glass down. On the kitchen table are my cassette tapes, my cassette player. All my things are there.

I can still use my hands in the daytime, still use them to type. I can still listen. I can still type. But when I listen and type I have the sense that it's somebody else doing the listening and the typing, that it's somebody else's hands performing the motions.

I tell myself that I would notice if somebody had been in my home, if somebody was following me on the street, if somebody was watching me. I don't feel watched. Just split in two. Half.

I undress and enter the bathroom. I wash my hands.

That's when I see it, something in my sink. I think it's a crack at first. But when I touch the crack with my finger it moves.

It's a hair.

I hold it in front of me.

I twist it around my finger and the tip of my finger grows hard, red, and swollen. The hair is pale, basically white, almost transparent, like a fishing line.

Does this belong to me? Has it been on my head? Did it fall from me?

Or is it somebody else's? Somebody who's been in my bathroom?

Whose is it now?

I twist the hair around my finger when I go to bed. I lie in bed and twist it around my finger, one, two, three times, and then I unspool it again. I listen to the silence.

When I wake up it's still dark, so I stay in my warm bed for a moment. I look out the window. I wait for dawn. I wait for the day to begin. It's morning, the digits on my alarm clock are glowing, but it's as dark as night. I've lost the strand of hair while sleeping. It's slipped off my finger. I don't see it anywhere.

Once dawn has broken I leave. I lock the door, double-checking to make sure it's really locked. I leave, I take the metro to the station with the yellow tiles, I walk up the stairs and then I get on the escalator. It's Sunday. There aren't a lot of people. A woman comes down the escalator, traveling in the other direction, downstairs, and she's holding on to the escalator's handrail, which moves a little faster than the escalator itself. She looks straight ahead with a vacant face. When we pass each other she corrects her grip, and I think to myself that her hand is beautiful. Long fingers.

I walk to the market. I pull my trench coat tighter. The air is cold and dry. They sell all kinds of things at the market: vegetables, clothes, kitsch. I look through the winter coats. A man nearby is smoking and drinking coffee from a paper mug. He's bald. He's dressed in black. He looks at me as I touch the coats with my ruddy, bare hands. They're good quality, he says. Good materials. I can tell, I can feel it with my hands. Who have all these coats belonged to? I ask him. Lots of people, he replies, brusque. He flings his cigarette to the ground and sucks on the coffee. I do estate sales, he continues. This is not some kind of trash. This is not some junk somebody wanted to get rid of. Nothing wrong with these. Good quality. Good materials. They've held up many years and will hold up many years yet.

He falls silent.

You look funny in that one, he says. That coat you're wearing. It's too big for you. Makes me think of...

He snaps his fingers.

You look like a detective. You look like a detective in an old movie.

I laugh to be polite. He clears his throat. His raspy laughter dies out. He lights a new cigarette.

I touch one of his coats. A camel-hair coat. It slides off the hanger easily when I touch it. The lining is slippery.

I put the coat on. It's warm.

That's a men's model, the man says.

Not an issue for me, I tell him. No, he says, that's true. He adjusts the collar. It fits you. It's not too big for you. It fits you perfectly.

I check the pockets with my bare hands. They're cool and pleasant. Roomy.

I'll take it, I say.

I buy it from the man. I don't take it off. He puts my trench coat in a yellow plastic bag.

I take the metro home. I lean my head against the window and close my eyes for a bit. I hold the yellow bag in my arms. My new coat smells a little. I can't say what exactly it smells of. Something old. Kind of fusty.

When I get home I open my kitchen window and put the camel-hair coat on a hanger in the window. I hang my old coat on another hanger and put it in the closet. Before I shut the closet door I put my hand in the pocket and take out my sheet of paper. I unfold it. I read the two sentences.

I have seen you. Have you seen me?

I fold the paper again and go to put it in the pocket of my new coat. When I stick my hand into the cool, slippery pocket I find something I didn't notice before. I didn't notice it on the market square. There's a tube in there. A heavy tube.

It's a lipstick.

I recognize it. I've seen the same golden textured tube in the department store. I've tried every brownish hue: BETTY, JUDY, DIANE, VERONIQUE...

I twist it to bring out the stick. It's a brown shade. The perfect shade. Exactly what I've been looking for. Why haven't I seen this shade before? Maybe it's gone out of production.

Pushing out the stick, I see that it's not a new lipstick, but old. Somebody has already used it. Used it until there's almost nothing left. Only a steep cut remains.

I put the stick against my lips, and to my surprise they don't give. My lips hold. I paint my lips. I go to the bathroom to check my own reflection. I look at my brown mouth. It's the only aspect of my face that's well-defined.

I turn the tube over, I read the name of the lipstick: LAURA.

I want to tell you. I'm going to. I just don't know where to begin.

KAROL AND LARISSA LIVE IN A BRICK BUILDING. YOU TAKE the elevator to their floor, a big, utilitarian, rattling freight elevator. Laura presses herself against the wall as they ride up. Are you scared of elevators? Naomi asks. Laura shakes her head. I used to be, Naomi says in a distracted tone. When I was little. I was claustrophobic. And scared of the dark. But I've never gotten trapped in an elevator, actually. Have you?

I don't know, Laura says.

She pushes a cuticle on one hand down with the other hand's thumbnail. Naomi sees a flake of nail polish fall. Mother-of-pearl varnish.

When did you paint your nails? Naomi asks. Yesterday, says Laura. After you went to work.

I didn't notice before, Naomi says.

It's a discreet shade, Laura says.

Naomi is cradling a bottle of wine. Laura is quiet, Naomi thinks to herself, and she herself feels anxious and irritable.

There's a moment of confusion when Naomi and Laura enter, but only a moment. Her friends are polite, they would never linger in their surprise at the sight of the other woman, this woman who looks like an odd, bad copy of Naomi, with the same hairstyle and the obviously home-dyed hair, and a practically identical camel-hair coat that she hangs on the same hook as Naomi's. Practically identical, as if she'd tried to dress up as Naomi, a practically identical coat that she labors a little too long to hang on the same hook as Naomi's, on top of Naomi's coat. They would never make a big deal out of any of it, not on purpose, they would never mention it, they would never want to make Laura uncomfortable by showing her that they've noticed, by openly displaying their surprise—but to hide it fully would be impossible, and they look at her with expressions they imagine to be curious, too polite to openly show that she makes them uncomfortable, that she makes them ill at ease, that they don't understand who she is and why Naomi has brought her here.

Naomi gives Karol a kiss on the cheek, and then Larissa. Laura shakes their hands. Laura, welcome, it's so nice to meet you, we've heard so much about you. Don't lie, Naomi says with a loud laugh, a little too forceful, as if she wanted to convey to Laura that this is the way she and her friends joke with each other, that this is what their tone is like, that they sometimes say things they don't mean, just for laughs. Naomi is sweating. Laura tugs at her sleeveless polo top, which is tight at the armpits. Her eyes dart around the room. I love your lipstick, Larissa says. How do you two know each other? Laura looks at Naomi and replies, in a terse voice, We're friends, and Naomi says, It's a funny story actually, it's a funny story, yeah, the way we know each other is that— it was an accident, soon after Christmas I had, well, it was by mistake, just an accident, that I took Laura's coat, and Larissa says, Right, you've got the same kind of coat, how funny, what a coincidence, but she doesn't quite understand the story or how this coincidence has led Naomi to bring this woman to her home. Gina is here, too, she says, and Gabriel, come say hi, and when Laura shakes their hands they all look at her, giving her their full attention, they look at her tight clothes, the bad dye-job, the stained hairline, the blotchy neck where the hair is unevenly cut, they see the sweat at her brow pushing through the makeup, and they see her insecure, darting eyes. Nobody has seen Naomi in weeks, and nobody understands what's going on with her, what she's doing, she seems strange, different, and now here she is, turning up with some kind of...

The walls of Karol and Larissa's living room are red. This is where they keep their dining table, a table in curly birch, and there's a bouquet of yellow tulips on the table, and their voices echo in the room. They need textiles—curtains, rugs, a thought Naomi has every time she's here. They open Naomi's wine. Why not, we'll start with this, it's a fun one. What is it? Chilean? Okay, do you hear the music? Do you recognize this melody? It's this funny record, a Gregorian choir, Gregorian monks, but they're singing pop songs, you hear it, right, if you listen? It's so funny to me, we bought it just because we were curious, almost like a joke, it just sounded too silly to me, but if I'm honest I'm actually quite into it, yes, I like to keep it on in the background, I listen to it all the time now...

Their wineglasses are thick and heavy, hand-blown with blue rims and small air bubbles stuck in the walls. Laura sinks back into the chair. She drinks from the wine. She listens. She watches as Naomi and her friends talk. She studies their faces. Larissa has dark hair, like

Naomi, maybe not quite as dark, and it's cut short with short, thin bangs. There's a mole under her lip, a fairly big dark mole that she keeps touching in a distracted, apparently compulsive gesture. Gabriel is bald, but his eyebrows are bushy, and the pores on his nose are dark and enlarged. Gina has a strong chin, square with a dimple, and a full mouth that seems to be constantly working somehow, it's always pouting a little, even when she's not talking, as if she has to struggle to take command of it, and her eyes are a little slanted, sort of hanging, they make her look kind of sad. Karol has short, curly hair, like a sheep, and he's got brown eyes; when she looks at him he suddenly turns his gaze on her and looks her right in the eye, and she lowers her gaze, focuses on the wineglass, an air bubble arrested in flight. But she feels his eyes on her. Feels him looking. She feels his eyes on her for what must be minutes.

There's a blue salad bowl on the table with chunky serving utensils in wood, and Larissa adds an orange casserole. I saw this recipe in the newspaper, I had to try it, I hope it's edible, I'm so bad at vegetarian food but of course Naomi doesn't eat meat, so this is something called something-something-*melanzane* and that's Italian, means eggplant.

Laura intermittently looks at Naomi, who is seated next to her. She glances at Naomi, she cuts her food, puts it in her mouth, chews, accepts when someone offers to top up her wineglass, and listens.

When did you stop eating meat? Did you never eat it? Is it about the taste or is it, like, what do you call it, is it a moral thing? Is it about your health? It's healthier to avoid meat, it's good, it's better to eat vegetables, olive oil is better, I read that somewhere, people live longer where they do that, that's what I heard, it's much better, not my family though, seriously, they're all over ninety and they smoke like chimneys and eat everything, butter and all kinds of things, and they drink, too. Wine is good for the heart, that's what they say, though I don't know if it's true. You live and you learn, right? But how do you get your nutrients? What about iron? Women need meat. What? Women need meat. Who says that? I don't know, it's something my mom used to say, I don't know if she had any evidence to back it up. Though I'm sure it's about the iron, don't you think, it's got to be about the iron. But there's iron in all kinds of things, spinach... In any case I don't think most kinds of meat are that nutritious, either, take mass-produced hot dogs, or what do you call it, that conserved ham thing— What are you talking about, it's not like we eat that? No, but I'm just saying, there's meat and then there's meat... Do you eat eggs? How about milk? Or honey, do you eat honey? Okay, here's a question: Would you rather drink milk from a pig or a rat? I know, horrible! But why do we drink milk from cows? And goats? Why doesn't that seem equally horrible? Is it about the taste? We eat pork, after all. Not me, I don't eat meat, as you know. No, no, I know, not you, but the rest of us. Oh my god, what a question. To drink milk from a pig. Or a rat! It's got to be the pig, no? Rat milk, milk from a rat, no, that sounds... I can't imagine it would be ... it just can't be sanitary, right, or what do you guys think? Okay, pigs are extremely clean animals. And we do eat their meat. Some of us. But I have to say, I can understand not wanting to eat pork, to me it feels, honestly, sometimes—I have to say, there's something about pigs, I've heard they're highly intelligent—and I've heard that human flesh resembles pork, actually, in terms of taste. No, that can't be true! Well, I don't know if it's true, but that's what I've heard. I just can't imagine it tastes like pork. Why not? It's got to be more bitter. I don't know why I think that, it's just a feeling. Have you ever tried milk abroad? It's got a different taste, don't you think? It's got a different taste, yes, it's not good, no, it's something totally different, entirely different. I think it's in the, what do you call it, it's something acquired, it's cultural, a thing of habit, to drink the kind of milk you were raised on. Listen, you know what's really terrible? It happened to me the other day. I picked up my water, but I took the wrong glass, I took Lou's glass instead, because it was on the counter, and I took this big sip, and it was milk! I thought I was going to die! I don't know why it grossed me out so much...I just wasn't prepared...Pig or rat... it's a horrible question, you're horrible to even think such a thought. Honestly, how could anybody answer that. Pig or rat...Wait, point of clarification: How much do you have to drink? Is it in proportion to the animal? What do you mean? I mean, if you pick the pig, does that mean you have to drink a big glass of milk, but if you pick the rat's milk a thimble is enough? Oh my god, that's an incredible question, so good...No, no, of course it's got to be the same amount, otherwise it's too easy...everyone would pick the rat...Yeah, to drink as little as possible...it's like taking medicine, you just close your eyes and... A whole glass though, no, what a disgusting thought... Right, it has to be the same amount, yes... okay, so how much? How much? A mouthful? What's that, like a good mouthful? A tablespoon? No, more than that, more than that! Oh, this conversation is so dumb, it's so, so dumb... So what do you want to talk about then? You could suggest something better instead of just complaining! We have to determine this before we can move on! Rat or pig! And how much? Fine, let's say you milk a rat or a pig and you pour it into a glass, and you have to take a big mouthful. You don't need to do more than one sip, but it has to be big. And what if it's delicious? Sure, you're free to drink the whole glass... I'm going to have to go with the pig... Pig... Pig... Rat... I'm curious... Okay, now that's settled we need to move on... I can't stand talking about this anymore... Are you easily grossed out? I am, actually, yes, it's something that's come with age, yes, since I turned forty I've gotten grossed out by, I don't know, things like using public bathrooms, touching doorknobs, or talking about this sort of thing when eating, I don't know, I don't know what it's about, maybe it's easier to imagine things as you get older... what do you guys think? Kids have no empathy, they're so selfish. You think so? When I was a child, oof, I was terrible... no, I don't think I had a lot of empathy... God, just don't tell us that you were tormenting animals! No, no, not like that—that's serial killer stuff, it wasn't that bad... Serial killer, really? In that case I guess I've got some of that in me because I definitely did that kind of stuff, pulling wings off flies and... Oh my god...

Excuse me, Laura says, and she gets up to use the restroom.

Naomi watches as she leaves, spinning her wineglass.

Your friend is nice, she's, what do you call it, elegant—yes, really—right—that was a funny story, that thing with your coats. Where was it? Ah, you like that place, don't you? I can see why, yes, I see that, a department store is a bit like an airport, outside of time. Oh come on, an airport, that's the least charming place in the world, how can you be romanticizing airports? And a department store? A place where you buy things? Airports, don't you think, what do you mean, it's romantic, of course it is... Yes, I'm with you... it's a place full of possibilities, don't you think? And people who meet and go their separate ways! You don't think so? Train stations, you don't think they're even a little bit romantic? Being on the way to somewhere? Well, I've already made my position clear, I don't like traveling at all. It's so unfair, you're the one who travels the most of us. But a department store, I seriously don't understand how that fits in here, in my world a department store is the most prosaic place, shopping, to me there's no beauty in that at all, none, nada.

The bathroom is at the end of a hallway, a small, windowless room with blue walls and a toilet, sink, and mirror, but no shower and no tub. It's clearly a guest bathroom, Laura thinks, there's no indication that it's used by anyone but guests. She shuts the door behind her. She hears the voices, though softly, over the music. She doesn't hear what they're saying, just the general sound.

On her way back she notices the door cracked open to Lou's room. She opens it, carefully, and enters. The child is sitting on the floor, drawing, and doesn't look up from the crayons when Laura shuts the door behind her and crouches on the floor. She clears her throat, but Lou doesn't move.

Do you mind if I sit here for a little while? she asks, and Lou nods.

She looks at the small hand, the yellow marker moving over the thin cartridge paper, back and forth. She looks at the walls, which have wallpaper on them, pale blue with daisies, and when she looks at them she's got a sense that she's seen this wallpaper before, though she can't remember where, or if she really has seen it at all. Maybe it reminds her of something she's seen in a movie, or read in a book. She adjusts her top, which keeps cutting into her armpits. It's too small. The top should be bigger or she should be smaller. She pushes her hair behind her ears and the oil makes her fingers sticky. Lou keeps moving the yellow marker intently across the paper. It's nice to sit here. She'll have to go back soon, and either way she's got the sense that Lou would prefer it if she left and is just too polite to say it.

Do you know Naomi? Laura asks, and for the first time Lou looks up from the drawing, and meets her gaze with a look of distaste. A dumb question. Still, the child nods.

I'm her friend, Laura says, and she receives no answer. Do you think we look alike?

No, Lou answers, firmly, and returns to the drawing.

Do you like drawing? she asks.

A nod.

Laura stays in the room for a little while longer. Then she gets up, leaves the room, shuts the door behind her, and returns to the table. Naomi's friends don't comment on her long absence when she sits down, they're too polite for that, but Karol watches as she sits down next to Naomi, when she briefly touches Naomi's neck.

After the guests have left he clears the table, drinks what's left of the wine, rinses the empty bottles and puts them in a bag for recycling, wipes the sink, throws out the full, heavy coffee filter. He grabs a toothpick. Naomi's friend, he says, Laura was her name? She looked at me—did you see that, too, did she look at you that way, too?—as if we'd met before. Do you know what I mean? She looked at me as if she recognized me. Did you notice that? I didn't notice that, Larissa says. Did you recognize her? No, Karol says, I couldn't place her for the life of me. When I opened the door and saw her I didn't know what to think. I thought I was seeing double.

He laughs and chews on his toothpick. Larissa laughs, too. Their laughter is polite and muted.

And then, he continues, when I got a better look at her, I only got more confused.

Yes, Larissa says. Yes. Me, too.

They actually do look alike.

You think so? Larissa says. I just couldn't take my eyes off that terrible haircut.

He laughs again. Yes. Yes, what was that about? It reeked of dye, Larissa says, her hair, it was recently done, this sharp smell, I know that smell from a mile away. It's some kind of artificial apricot fragrance they use to try to bury the chemicals in. And did you see her neck? The hair was totally uneven in the back. But I don't know. Maybe I'm making too big of a thing out of it. Yes. I don't know, either. She was quiet. Didn't say much. No, Karol says, she didn't say much. Nothing, Larissa continues, she said nothing all night, basically. Right? No, Karol says, now that you mention it I can't recall her saying a single word all night. Some prefer to listen, I guess, Larissa says. Maybe we should have been nicer to her. Should we? Were we rude? Should we have asked more questions? I guess we can be a bit loud sometimes. It's easy to forget. I imagine it can make a new person feel excluded. Maybe we should have asked more questions. But I don't know ... I was so distracted by the whole ... Did Naomi tell you that she was bringing a guest? Yeah, she did, actually. She mentioned it on the phone. I didn't think to ask any follow-up questions. No, why would you have done that? Right, exactly. No, it was just strange. It was just strange.

Karol throws his toothpick in the trash.

Well, he says. Stranger things have happened.

On the metro, Laura leans her head against the train's window, and Naomi, in the seat across from her, does the same. She's a little tipsy. She's not eaten properly today, not enough to guzzle all that wine, all she had was a boiled egg for breakfast. She looks at the flashing white light of the lamps in the tunnel. Both of them feel ill at ease, but in different ways and without being able to talk about it. They get off at the station with the yellow tiles. On the way up to the street they pass a busker playing the accordion. Lambada. He's using a microphone, which causes the melody to ricochet between the walls. They walk homeward in silence, pulling their coats tighter in the evening chill. Naomi pushes her door open and they slowly climb the five flights of stairs, pausing at every landing to catch their breath. Naomi drops her keys on the floor when they get inside. She goes to bed immediately, without removing her makeup. Laura enters the bathroom and turns on the lights, and then she looks at her face in the mirror, scrutinizing, touching it, touching the hairline, and the eyes.

If there's one thing in my life I can feel proud of, it's the fact that I have—and essentially on my own, too—the fact that I've raised two sons, my children. That's something I can feel proud of. That I've done that. I did a good job with it. Peter, I was never concerned about him, though every once in a while Fredrik gave me reason to worry. He could get so angry. He grew big and wide, bigger than his dad, I mean, he was tall, and yes, sort of big, and he would get so angry. So angry. I don't know why. No, I don't know why . . . I don't know why . . . I don't know—why him? There's one time in particular. Do I need to tell you about it? Yes. Yes, I'll try. I'll tell you. I want to try. I will. But the main thing . . . the main thing is that I raised my sons to be good people, and that they're happy and healthy. That's all I ever wanted. It was the only thing. Long before they were even born.

But that's different from what's actually mattered to me. I mean that . . . I meant . . . when I talk about what matters . . . I talk about what I did, and what I wish I would have done. Yes, what I've spent my time thinking about, and what I wish I would have spent my time thinking about. As a young person I was so concerned for the world, for the world around me, for the lives of other people . . . I wanted everyone to be alright . . . I had a lot of . . . compassion . . . for poor people . . . when I myself was living so comfortably. And I wanted to help people who weren't as lucky as me. I wanted so badly to help them. As a child I was sometimes brought to tears over someone else's misfortune. Someone who didn't get to have a life . . . where they could be their best self . . . ah, I'm trying to find the right words. What I mean is . . . not just those with terrible fates . . . war and starvation . . . illness . . . but anyone who had the slightest . . . I'm not explaining myself well. But this was how I felt as a child. That the world's pain was on my shoulders. While I got to play and be happy. We lived in a big house with a garden, it was a dream, that garden, a true paradise for a child. I'd walk from bush to bush, picking flowers just for the pleasure of picking them, and then I was scolded afterward for ruining the plants. I didn't do a nice job picking them, it wasn't to make a bouquet. I tore the petals from the roses . . . I liked the feeling when they came loose. I liked how soft the petals felt against my fingers. It was a happy childhood. But I spent so much time thinking about other people and their misfortunes, which I read about in books. And I thought that when

I grew older I would dedicate my life to helping these unfortunate people. Who were . . . outside my garden . . . I thought that was the meaning of life. But when I got older I saw . . . it was easier for a child to care about other people's misfortune. Because as a child you can't actually do anything about it, just weep. And when I was older . . . It pains me to say this . . . it was too hard. There were other things that called me. I didn't understand, as a child, that you have to sacrifice something in order to help others. And I wanted to live a comfortable life. I valued that over helping others. Yes. Of course I didn't understand it at the time, that I was making a choice. That I was turning my back on the less fortunate . . . that I was putting myself first. Sometimes I had this jolt, this feeling that I'd betrayed my ideals. Whatever they were. But every time I let myself be distracted again. By delicious food and nice clothes. I was so young when I married! My husband was older, almost twenty years older! He often told me, Sweet child! He loved that I thought so much about the poor and unfortunate. And I loved that he loved it . . . he thought I was a good person . . . that was enough for me . . . him thinking I was a good person. And our friends would say, Oh, you're so sensitive! You can't even watch the news without crying . . . yes, that's how I took in the world, like a child. Without doing anything about it. I just cried . . . and it felt good to cry . . . but in truth, of course I knew...yes, soon I'm going to have to...I need to return to my childhood again. I'll do that later. So you have something to write in the book...a few details...By the way, don't include any of this. I don't want everyone to know. This is what I want you to say: I've always felt deeply about other people's suffering. I've had that empathy ever since I was a child. I was born this way and I will die this way. With great empathy—even though I myself have lived such a simple and comfortable life—for all those unfortunate souls whose lives are difficult.

I was supposed to have a twin sister. She was stillborn. They couldn't say why...it's not that uncommon...it's not uncommon for one twin to not survive...and though I understand, intellectually, that it's silly to think like this, I've never quite been able to shake the feeling that it's my fault...or that it was, somehow, a mistake that I lived and she didn't...that I took her place on Earth...

Ah. I had a patient who put her hands around my throat! It wasn't a very strong grip, it was a girl of, well, how old would she have been, in her twenties maybe, though she looked like a teenager—but it scared me! I really did think for a moment that I was going to die! All my life I've had violent nightmares about the ceiling of my bedroom caving in, trapping me in there, like a little... and if this were to happen to me, how afraid I'd be then—and how disappointed I'd be, to realize I'd had a prophetic dream all my life and then not be able to tell anyone...

After our wedding we moved to this apartment, it's beautiful, with a view of a tree-lined street. The trees were smaller back then but by now they've grown big, and it's one of the great joys of my life to stand beneath those trees and smell their fragrance in the spring... but I was thinking... I keep getting sidetracked... After our wedding we moved to this beautiful apartment. I bought lots of art, I wanted to cover the walls with art, art is what I've always lived for, it's what makes life worth living, and it's one of the great joys of my life to walk through the rooms of my home and look at all the art we bought, the things we've collected, everything that makes life beautiful... this beautiful, beautiful apartment with big windows, lots of natural light, French balconies, it was a dream come true to move into this apartment. Yes. What else can I tell you... oh, we had a garage, yes, a garage...

I GET ON THE METRO BEFORE THE SUN IS UP, I STAMP MY ticket, BANG, I stand up in the clattering train, I listen to the chiming of the doors. I pull my coat closer. It's warm and soft. I've painted my lips with LAURA. When I look at myself in the train window, when I look at my own reflection in the scratched window, the window that shakes in the tunnel, my wide, pursed, brown mouth is the only aspect that's clearly defined. My face is pale, diffuse, my eyes are nothing but two holes, my head is like smoke. But the mouth is sharp, I can see the mouth in the window, I see it clearly, and I taste the mouth, my painted mouth, the stale, sweet taste of old makeup.

Does the lipstick belong to a dead person, too? I guess it's not impossible. It's probably likely.

I get off at the old station, walk past the open phone booth and the photo booth, walk down the stairs. I walk through the darkness to the ghostwriter's office. It smells like fire.

The ghostwriter has never given me any time off. No more than a couple of days. Nor has the ghostwriter ever taken more than a couple of days off from work himself. What would that look like?

No, somebody has to do what we do. Somebody has to listen. And somebody has to write.

So even though I'm disappearing, even though I feel halved, I go to pick up my tapes from the ghostwriter.

We drink a little cup of coffee. He compliments my lipstick.

It suits you, he says.

I go home. I get to work. I sit with my hands prone. I listen.

Sometimes the ghostwriter makes things up. He confesses this to me.

We're having dinner together at the Chinese restaurant. We're at the table by the street-facing window, the window with red lanterns and green plants in terracotta pots. The window is fogged up. Nothing is visible outside, nothing is clearly visible, all we see are hazy shadows of people hurrying by and the white and red lights of the cars. The door keeps opening and closing next to us. The bell chimes. Customers come in and sit at the bar while they wait for their food, groups come in and sit down at their tables. We drink beer. The bottle is green with condensation on it. It's ice-cold. I eat and eat. My tongue is numb. My lipstick has come off, I've eaten it, and I no longer feel it at the contours of my lips though I know it's there, an ugly brown line. I'd like to fix it when I get a chance. But for now we're eating.

You look worn out, the ghostwriter says.

He drinks from his bottle and I drink from my bottle. We eat and eat. I don't respond, but I don't think he's expecting a reply. I know he's right. I do look worn out.

The ghostwriter looks pretty worn out himself. Not at all so boyish, I'm realizing. His cheeks are sunken. His hair is matted. He works a lot. He works day and night.

Sometimes I make things up, he says. Sometimes I

just have to do it. Sometimes reality bores me. It's not something I ever set out to do, no, it's rarely something I plan. No, it's not something I decide to do. I don't have an agenda. But I do it anyway. I write about things that never happened. I can't help it. Sometimes you just need to stretch the truth a bit. Have some fun.

He burps and immediately puts a hand in front of his mouth, clearing his throat as if trying to give the impression that this is what he did.

I've made up quite a lot of things, he says. I have to admit, there's quite a number of things I've made up. Lost in thought, he gazes out the foggy window. An ambulance drives past. We hear the wail of the sirens. Sometimes it needs something, he says, something more, a little spice, a little color. Yes, I say.

And it doesn't really matter, does it? the ghostwriter says. If you stretch the truth a bit sometimes. No, I say.

After all, the books are called Story of a Life, the ghostwriter says. Not The Truth of a Life. Right, I say.

And not, the ghostwriter says—something excited in his eyes now—The Story of a Life. Right, I say. Do you understand the difference? he asks. Yes, I say. Story, the ghostwriter says, not The Story. In other words, this is one story among many possible stories. Not the final, singular story.

I chew and swallow. I nod. It's true.

Is this story true? the ghostwriter asks. I'll leave that unsaid.

There are clients who get back in touch with the ghostwriter after they've received the red book, wanting to commission another. The ghostwriter always says no. You only get one chance. He always says no, regardless of the reason they want him to write another book. Since the ghostwriter only agrees to write one story per client it is, in a way, final. But I don't have the energy to debate this with him.

He digs in the rice bowl using the white ceramic spoon. We eat in silence for a moment.

I don't know who has inspired him to think about these things. I wonder if one of his clients complained that he stretched the truth too far. After all, they pay to receive a story about their own lives. They don't pay to read a novel by the ghostwriter. He's not an author. And they're not characters in a novel. They're real people. They offer up their lives to the ghostwriter. They need to be able to trust him.

And in any case, the ghostwriter says, some of them are so...

He trails off.

Some just go on and on, he continues. Some only share things that don't . . . things that are completely useless for my work . . . you know that better than anyone else . . .

Yes, I say.

It flatters me when the ghostwriter speaks like this. When he insinuates that I know better than anybody what his work is like. What the women are like. How vague they can be. How boring. How they sometimes walk in circles around absolutely pointless things, pointless details, how they never get to the heart of the matter. I know better than anybody how little they understand about themselves, how little they understand what is interesting about their lives, what is important, how little weight they give to the details that are meaningful to the ghostwriter and, therefore, also to themselves. They know so little about themselves. They don't know what their lives are about. I know better than anybody else how they need to be reminded, again and again, to talk about life as it truly was, to tell their story in concrete terms, in specific terms, tell it without reservation, without irony and without putting their guard up. They have to be reminded to tell it straight, tell the truth, so that the ghostwriter can lie in their place, so the ghostwriter can turn their life into art, so that they, thanks to the ghostwriter, can have eternal life.

The ghostwriter drinks from his bottle again and gesticulates to the server. He holds up our empty rice bowl, then turns to me. Another beer? I nod. The ghostwriter chews and looks out the window. I follow his gaze, but see nothing out there, no shadow of a person, no lights. We receive a new bowl of rice, a steaming lacquered bowl, and two green bottles. We clink.

You look worn out, he says.

You already said that, I say.

I did? he says. Yes, maybe I did. Are you sleeping poorly?

I nod. I haven't slept in several weeks, I say. And barely eaten, either.

That's physiologically impossible, the ghostwriter says and drinks from his bottle. You'd be dead by now.

We've got a lot of work, I say.

The ghostwriter cracks his fingers. Don't work yourself to death, he says.

No, I say.

The ghostwriter has written hundreds of books. I don't understand how he does it. I'm tired just from transcribing the women's recordings. My hands and my head are tired. I could never write and think at the same time. I need the voice that tells me what to type. I need to know what to do. I only know how to listen. I only know how to write exactly what they say. I can't organize a life the way he can. I just can't.

Some of the women who contact the ghostwriter and ask him to write a new book do it because they're unhappy with their red book and want a new, better version. They realize there were things they forgot to share. They want the narrative to emphasize other things. Others, I think, just miss being close to the ghostwriter. And being close to themselves. I think they miss the work of recording themselves while they talk. Without interruption. The red book helps them see themselves. It helps them understand that they've existed. It helps them die.

I look out through the foggy window and see nothing. The fog is like a wall. I can't see out, and I can't see the reflection of the restaurant, nor my own reflection. I check for the sheet of paper in the pocket of the coat that hangs from my seatback.

Something strange happened to me recently, I say, and I look at the ghostwriter.

He looks at me with a serious expression, his gaze direct. He folds his hands and holds them still. He listens. I can see why his way of listening inspires the women to trust him.

I heard something that scared me. I heard something I didn't understand. And since then I've had a sense of being split in two.

The ghostwriter nods and holds my gaze.

It's as if I were double, I say. I have this feeling that part of me has left me but continues to exist somewhere else. And I feel as if I am gradually disappearing. I've started to lose my reflection. My face is like mud. It doesn't hold.

The ghostwriter is silent.

No, he says, eventually. It's true. You're right. You've become diffuse. You sort of lack color.

And I have a hard time remembering things, I say. For instance, how long have I worked for you?

The ghostwriter shakes his head. I can't remember, either. Feels like you've been working for me since the dawn of time.

Yes, I say. That's what it feels like to me, too.

I don't know how I managed before, he says. I actually don't remember. It feels as if we've always worked together.

We fall silent, listening to the cars that pass by outside the window. The bell rings again. A woman enters the restaurant and orders at the bar. Food for take-out. She sits down and waits with her chin resting in her hand. I see the ghostwriter look at her. I look at her. We only see the back of her head, but the back of her head is attractive, with dark, shiny hair. She's got the same kind of coat as me. A similar coat. A camel-hair coat.

I think you have to let go, he says, and he turns back to me. I think you have to move on.

But how? I say.

The ghostwriter shrugs, and he grabs a toothpick and starts digging around in his mouth.

Well, what do you say, he says. Tomorrow is another day.

He asks for the bill. He pays. The receipt arrives on a small ceramic plate, alongside two mints. The ghostwriter takes one of the mints and puts it in his pocket. I put the other one in my mouth. I toss it back and forth with my tongue so that it hits my teeth, I suck on it until it becomes a slim shard. At the metro we go our separate ways. I feel like taking a walk, the ghostwriter says.

I stand in place and watch him leave. I watch him disappear.

WALKING TO THE METRO, NAOMI SLIPS HER HANDS INTO her coat pockets and feels, in one of them, a folded, coarse piece of paper. She doesn't recognize it. She doesn't know what it is. Trash, probably. She takes it out as she walks down the stairs, she's moving at a fast clip, familiar with the steps and not worried about stumbling, she unfolds the piece of paper. It's a regular thin sheet of printer paper with two sentences at the top: I have seen you. Have you seen me?

This has no meaning for her. She doesn't know how this piece of paper ended up in her pocket. She puts it back. Then she buys a ticket and stamps it, BANG, and she spends the ride cleaning her nails with the sharp edge of the paper ticket. Somebody has spilled coffee in the center aisle of the train. Not one single puddle but many little ones, like a comet's tail. The white light of the lamps in the tunnel hits one of the puddles and creates a reflection, and throughout her ride the coffee puddle and the train blink in tandem, first quickly and then slower and slower as it decelerates to stop at a station. When she gets off she throws her used ticket into a trash can. She tosses the sheet of paper, too, while she's at it. It's nothing she needs to keep.

She's bored at work. She drinks a little cup of coffee. She chats with Felix at the watercooler. This time of year I never know how to dress, he says, you leave the house in the morning and there's practically frost on the ground, but the afternoons are too warm for a winter coat. Still, I could never live somewhere without seasons, I know that for sure, yes, I love it when the seasons change. I haven't forgotten your book, by the way, it's in my office—wait here and I'll get it. I'm so curious to hear what you think.

He leaves and quickly returns with a slender little red book. She takes it from him and opens it, flipping through the pages without reading. Thanks, Felix. She puts it away, making sure she'll remember to bring it home.

On her lunch break she takes a little walk in the radio house park instead of eating. She strolls leisurely around the pond. The water has a musty smell, but she likes that smell, the smell of water in the city. There's a reflection of the sky in the pond, but to see the actual sky she has to tilt her head back, because the park is surrounded by tall buildings that block the view and leave the park in shade. Today, the sky is white. She checks with her thumbnail and finds that her middle finger is a little tender under the nail. She went too far earlier, to where the nail is attached to the skin, like—this is what she pictures—a snail attached to its shell. Today she's neither happy nor unhappy. The brown soil is dotted with green lances, and soon there's going to be little flowers, crocuses or something like it. It's practically speaking spring already, she thinks, it can't be more than days off now. The air is chilly, yes, but not like in winter. There's a concert tonight, which means she'll be at the radio house until late, and the thought of Laura being alone in the apartment for so long makes her uncomfortable. It's a new feeling. She can't say what she's worried about. All she knows is that she doesn't like it.

Late that evening she's on her way home, she's walking to the metro when it begins to rain. She's got no umbrella and there's no point in trying to protect herself from the rain with her coat. She buys a ticket and pays with lots of little coins, a short line forming behind her. She stamps her ticket and holds it in her hand as she gets on the train. When she distractedly begins to poke at her nails with it she stops and squeezes it in her hand instead. The metro car is humid and warm, there's condensation on the window and it smells of wool, perfume, sweat, and mouth. It rains when she gets off the metro, it rains for the duration of her short walk home, her hair gets wet and her face, too, she squints, and through her eyelashes she makes out the green and red reflection of traffic lights on the wet concrete. Cars drive by and splash water onto the sidewalk. She tosses her used ticket, which is all soft and limp by now, into a trash can. Right then she realizes that the book, Felix's book, is gone, and she can't recall when she last had it. She's sure she didn't leave it at the radio house. Maybe she left it on the train, or in the station, or earlier than that, sometime during the evening, somewhere in the concert hall, but she's not sure. She repines. She feels unexpectedly upset about this loss and the thought that she's going to have to explain to Felix that she's lost his book. If I'm lucky he'll forget about it, she thinks, trying to banish the thought from her mind. It's a problem for later. Maybe it won't even become a problem.

Even as she puts her key in the lock, as she unlocks the door, before she's even had time to open it, Laura, in the dark, stands from her chair. She gives Naomi a kiss on the mouth. Did you go outside today? Naomi asks. No, Laura says.

It's late. They drink a glass of wine in the kitchen.

Laura's hair looks matte, Naomi thinks. It annoys her. It's got no shine whatsoever, she thinks, and the thought makes her instinctively run her own hand through her own smooth, shiny hair, her naturally dark hair, which just grows like this, straight out of her scalp. Laura doesn't take care of her hair, Naomi thinks. She doesn't care for her hair the way Naomi does. It's not just that it's been dyed. It's also that it's dry and unruly, probably because she uses too much shampoo. Furthermore, the dye looks unnatural, it's even more obvious now in the light of the kitchen lamp: it's far too red. The dye stains on her scalp and neck are gone, but instead, just a week later, her roots are showing. There's a pale shadow over her scalp that makes her look bald. It annoys Naomi. She holds on hard to the stem of her wineglass, feeling the nail on her middle finger throb. It's like a stye, but in the wrong place. And those eyebrows, she thinks, are way too pale. They don't match her hair. And she looks tired, flabby, and dumb. Isn't she holding her wineglass kind of weirdly? Kind of wrong?

Laura doesn't seem to notice Naomi's scrutiny, and this irritates her further. She looks at Laura's hands and sees that the mother-of-pearl varnish is almost entirely gone. Her cuticles are ugly. Naomi can tell she's been biting them.

You don't take care of your appearance, Naomi says,

in a brusque voice. Laura looks at her with as blank of an expression as she can muster. She doesn't want Naomi to understand how much the comment hurts. Naomi interprets it as nonchalance. It's like speaking to a deaf person, or a wall. The vacant look infuriates her. It makes her want to say something truly scathing, but she can't think of anything to say and Laura doesn't respond, either. I mean, what do you think? Naomi asks. Would you say that you take care of your appearance? No, Laura says. I don't know.

Look at me, Naomi says, and look at yourself.

Laura doesn't answer.

She knows Naomi is right.

She knows that she looks like a bad copy of her.

She needs to do something different.

In the morning Naomi makes coffee and boils eggs. She regrets her own meanness, but isn't sure how to broach the subject. Laura is still silent. Her hair is messy. She peels an egg but isn't very hungry. She peels an orange, and the color and smell stick to her chipped nail polish. Naomi blows on her coffee and reads the newspaper. Her nails, Laura thinks, are near-perfect ovals. The radio is on. It's the requests hour, and they listen as an old woman's voicemail is played. I'd like to hear something that puts you in a good mood, she says, I'd appreciate that greatly, and once she's stopped talking, the fourth movement of Beethoven's Ninth Symphony begins. Laura chews on her orange slice and licks her fingers.

She finally plucks up her courage and takes Naomi's

hand. Do you think, Laura says, that you might want to help me?

They walk to the supermarket together. Naomi grabs a basket. They've never been there together, and it's a situation that brings her happy associations. She'd almost forgotten what it's like to go grocery shopping with someone. It's been a long time since she did that. It's not something she thought she was missing. They walk past the fruits and the vegetables, the pyramids of apples, onions, oranges, and bell peppers, they walk straight past the bread. They walk directly to the aisle with hygiene and beauty products. Naomi puts a roll of cotton rounds in the basket, she's almost out of those. And Q-tips, why not, they're always good to have. Then they stand in front of the shelves of hair dyes for a long time, trying to decide. Laura picks up one of the boxes and holds it in front of them. Naomi shakes her head and takes another one, much darker in color. She holds it next to her head, and Laura compares Naomi's hair to the full mane of the model. See? Naomi says. It's almost black, okay? There shouldn't be the slightest hint of red. Laura nods. Not the slightest hint of red.

Naomi gets a box of eyebrow dye, too, and on their way to the registers, Laura impulsively adds a bottle of sparkling water to the basket. The bottle is green.

When they get home, Naomi brings Laura to the bathroom, sets her down on a chair, and combs her hair with the pretty tortoiseshell comb. She wraps a towel around Laura's shoulders, the same towel Laura used, the pale-yellow one, the ruined towel, with dark, rust-colored stains all over it. It's obvious when you look at the stains, Naomi thinks, that she picked the wrong color.

She cuts the hair at Laura's neck. She makes it even and straight. Then she puts on the plastic gloves that come with the box, mixes the dye in a little bowl, and applies it to Laura's hair, a bit at a time, with the little brush that also came with the box. She works diligently and carefully, making sure that the dye doesn't touch the skin around the hairline or on the neck. The dye's strong scent almost makes her sneeze. It reminds her of a type of yogurt she used to eat as a child, a perfectly smooth yogurt with a completely made-up taste of peach or apricot.

While they wait for the dye to work, Naomi puts on the duduk CD, and Laura opens the bottle of sparkling water and pours a glass. She brings it to the bathroom and gives it to Naomi. Naomi rinses off the dye in the tub. Laura wraps her hair in a new towel, a red one. Naomi mixes the eyebrow dye with a few drops of hydrogen peroxide and applies it with a little brush. Laura looks funny with the color on her eyebrows, like somebody has drawn an angry face on her.

But when she wipes off the excess dye with a pair of cotton rounds, when she lets her wet hair down, they're both shocked by the results. The difference is enormous. The dyed eyebrows have a bigger effect than the hair. They make her face look sharper, her gaze clearer. Were it not for the pale eyes, Naomi thinks, it would be easy to confuse us for each other. They stand in front of the mirror and look at each other for a long while.

Naomi throws out the stained cotton rounds, cleans

the sink and the tub, and washes her hands. Meanwhile, Laura takes a new cotton round, soaks it in acetone, and removes what's left of the ugly old nail polish. She washes her hands, which turn bright red from the hot water and her vigorous rubbing with the soap, and then she goes to sit in the kitchen, letting her loose hair dry naturally. The sun floods in over the kitchen table and shines on the glass coffeepot with the nearly dried-up dregs, the empty cups, on the plates with eggshells and orange peels and the bowl full of oranges, the fruit flies and the newspaper that hangs over the edge of the table. The radio is on. She spreads her fingers and shakes the bottle of nail polish. The varnish is a little thick, but she paints slowly, and the end result is good. It looks even, pretty. She screws the cap back on and sits with her fingers spread, looking out the window, at the building next door and the tree in the yard, waiting for the varnish to dry. She blows on her fingers. She has the thought, a thought that makes her feel elated, that she's currently experiencing a pleasant morning in Naomi's life. A morning that Naomi must have experienced herself. A morning where she cares for her appearance.

Naomi enters the kitchen and inspects the nails. Good.

Once the polish is diamond-hard, Laura puts on Naomi's black turtleneck sweater, her black pants, her earrings, and her perfume. Naomi takes a bit of oil from the bottle and applies it to Laura's hair, then hooks the hair behind her ears. She carefully applies eyeliner to Laura's eyelids. She puts the dye boxes, the stained plastic gloves, and the brushes in a trash bag and ties the flaps. They put on their coats. Standing in front of the hall mirror, Laura paints her lips with the brown lipstick. Come here, she tells Naomi, hold on, and she opens the stick and grabs Naomi's chin. Open. She paints her lips.

They look at each other in the hall mirror. It's perfect.

I could be your doppelgänger now, Laura says. She puts her cheek against Naomi's cheek. She's a little taller and has to bend slightly. All that's left is the eyes, Naomi says. What can we do about that?

She kisses Laura and thinks that it's like kissing herself.

They take a walk together, along the canal, arm in arm. Naomi pushes her free hand deep into her rough coat pocket. They go to the department store. They pull the heavy doors open and enter the warm interior. It's bustling in there, beige marble, mirrors, chrome and glass, the hum of voices. They take the escalator. The department store is decorated with yellow bows and paper daffodils. They take the escalator one floor up (women's fashion, bags, and accessories), and Naomi picks out a pair of sunglasses. Black glass, black frames. She buys one pair for Laura and one for herself. If their eyes are hidden, she figures, the costume will be complete.

They're wearing the sunglasses when they continue up to the fifth floor, to the café, and they keep them on while they drink an espresso each. Laura eats a little chocolate that costs her nothing, while Naomi leaves hers on the plate.

She takes Laura's hand and holds it in her lap, looking around to see if anybody has noticed them, if anybody is surprised by the sight of them, this sight of two apparently identical women sitting there together. She feels elated at the thought of the sight, and over this budding sensation, which she can't quite put into words, there's a sense of unease, a question she can't ask, a question she can't ask Laura but not herself, either: Why does Laura want them to look like each other? Is it an erotic fixation? Is it some kind of mental illness?

But at night she whispers, with her lips pressed to Laura's pink, smooth earlobe, that she thinks they've got the same soul, that she's sure of it now, that she already knew it the first time they met, the first time she looked into her eyes. She whispers that when she looked into Laura's eyes she could see straight into her, and that when she did she was looking straight into millions of years of having existed as dust in this world, together, as one and the same rock, fly, or person—don't you think so, she whispers, don't you think so? She turns to Laura, putting them eye to eye, and she looks into Laura's pupil, looks at her own small distorted face. Don't you think? Yes, Laura responds, for the first time. Yes, I think so, I do believe that.

At night, though sleep is slow to arrive, Laura doesn't get up. This time she stays in bed with her belly against Naomi's back, with her arm around Naomi's chest.

Every morning she gets up and combs her hair, combs it carefully, and when she goes outside she hides her pale eyes behind the sunglasses. She greets Naomi's neighbors when she sees them in the stairwell, and they greet her. Hello, Naomi, good morning. She walks along the canal, she walks to Rigardi and drinks a cup of coffee, she walks to the department store and whiles away the time, she walks through the world like a new person—yes, she feels like a new person, increasingly she feels like a new person, as if she's been given a new life, and there are even moments when she forgets it's a costume, moments when she has the sense of being one with it; it's as if what Naomi whispers at night really is true, it's as if they move through the world as one.

She's at home one day, alone, when the phone rings. At first she hesitates, but then she does it. She picks up the phone. She makes her voice a little deeper. It's Karol. How nice of you to call, she says, how lovely to hear your voice. He's not calling about anything in particular, he's just calling to chat. He's at home, bored. He's supposed to be writing a play. It's about an unsolved murder, but he's gotten stuck doing research and the more he reads, the more he delays the work. You know what it's like. Sometimes you just need to jump in, Laura says, let your hands do the work and not think so much. What are you doing at home this time of day? I'm glad you picked up, I called on a whim. Ah, Laura says, I've been kind of sick, I've been home for a few days, but I'm starting to feel better, at this point I'm just lying around, feeling bored. Yes, Karol says, now that you say it I can hear there's something with your voice. It's the season. Everyone is sick this time of year. Thanks so much for a lovely dinner, by the way, Laura says. I need to have you guys over soon. When I'm feeling better. Would love that, Karol says. Or you can come over to us someday.

I'm home most of the time, you know, you can just ring the doorbell. You're welcome whenever you want. You're most welcome to come distract me. I'm always ready to be distracted. It was nice to have you over, it was nice to meet your ... Laura, your friend. Ah, Laura says, her, yeah, actually I wanted to apologize about that. I think you might have found her a little strange. Oh no, not at all, Karol says emphatically. It's okay, you can say it, Laura says, and he doesn't reply. She basically invited herself, Laura says. She's one of those people you can't get rid of. We met by chance, you know, it was this funny coincidence. Right, Karol says, I didn't quite understand how it came about, to be honest. He laughs. No, Laura says and laughs, me neither. But you know what it's like with people like that. You meet somewhere and all of a sudden they show up wherever you go, you just can't get rid of them. If I'm being completely honest with you, I think she's a little bit in love with me. Right, Karol says, I sort of did sense that. She says things to me, Laura says, that are totally, I don't know how to put it, that seem almost religious. She thinks we've been the same person in another life. That we're made of the same matter. That's the sort of things she says. I've stopped seeing her, though. Now I avoid her when she gets in touch. We don't talk anymore. I think she's a little crazy, actually. I have to admit, if I'm being totally honest with you, that she kind of scares me.

YELLOW AIR STREAMS OUT OF THE METRO, THERE'S THE sound of an accordion—Lambada—and the melody echoes between the walls. BANG. I take a seat, I sit with my forehead against the cool window. In the window I see, in the reflection, that there's an issue of CITY on the seat next to mine. There's a big, black headline on the front page: MURDER! I turn around. I open the paper. It's difficult to focus on the text. The letters seem blurry, the ink sooty. I fold the paper again. I set it down with the big, black headline facing the seat. My hands are soiled from touching it.

I get off the train, walk up the stairs, and then the escalator. There aren't a lot of people out. I walk through the underpass. It's dark and reeks of piss. My steps echo between the shiny, tiled walls. I get out into the cold, fresh air and fill my lungs.

I enter Rigardi and ask for a glass of water. I sit down at the bar. It's crowded in here. My hands are shaking. My vision is blurry. I have to hold the glass the bartender gives me with both hands to move it to my lips, but when I drink the water tastes weird. It's sweet. I spit it out.

This is milk, I say. The bartender says nothing. He is wiping glasses with a red-and-white checkered cloth. He's wearing a hat that says DADDY'S LITTLE DADDY.

I asked for a glass of water, I say.

Milk is better with spicy food.

Perhaps he's right, but now I've spat into the glass. Now I don't want it anymore.

I look around the bar, look at the floor, the blinking slot machines, CINZANO, the lacquered, reddish door that swings back and forth. Someone must have just come in through that door. Or out from it. I blink to clear my vision, but it's still blurry. It's hazy inside Rigardi, dark and hazy. Most likely, I think, it's the cigarette smoke. Yes, it's the smoke. That's why my vision is blurry. It's not that my eyes have some kind of problem, it's not my head. That's why I can't see the other people at Rigardi properly. That's why I see them as shadows, hazy outlines, background shapes. That's why I see my own face in the mirror behind the bar as a pale blob, a diffuse silhouette. Nobody takes notice of me.

The glass of milk is still on the bar, with my thick, bubbly spit floating on the surface. I've got the sweet, sticky taste in my mouth. I suck on my teeth. I rest my chin in my hands. I feel sleepy. A pleasant feeling. When I'm sleepy I don't feel anxious.

I calm down.

Eventually I put a few coins on the bar and leave, stepping into the cold outside. It's snowing again. Not a beautiful snowfall. This is an ice-cold, frigid sleet that melts before it hits the ground. The asphalt is black and wet. The snow gets to my bones. The streetlights are hazy; the red, green, yellow, and white streetlights and the lights of the cars and the lights from the roaring buses, and the hands, my naked hands, they look blurry when I put them out and spread my fingers. I check my pockets for my gloves. I put them on. It's the snow, I tell myself, it's because of the snow. It's the weather. The snow is what's making everything blurry, like a chilly fog. I walk home with my eyes on the ground, my eyes on the feet that carry me. I walk with my eyes on the ground until I arrive at my door, the narrow door, and I fumble to find the keyhole before I manage to get the door open, and then I walk across the yard, past the trash cans, up all five flights of stairs in my freezing stairwell, and I unlock the door to my apartment, clumsy in the dark. I take off my gloves but I leave the coat on. I pull it closer. I lie down on my bed, still dressed. I check my pocket for the tube, it's cold and heavy, I hold it in my hand, feeling its weight with my hand. I touch my piece of paper. I listen to the silence. My eyes are open but I can barely see anything in the murky room. After a while I shut my eyes.

I hear all the little sounds, the water in the radiators, the whirring of the fridge, the muted sound of traffic finding its way in through the walls and windows. I listen for sounds from my neighbors, their voices or their steps, but there's nothing. They must be asleep. I imagine them sleeping. I try to rein in my terror by listening. I cling to this moment of being alive. The feeling of my heavy head on the pillow. The feeling of the rough piece of paper I'm touching and the slippery lining of my pocket. My breathing.

I try to recall my life. The life I had before I heard the whisper. Before I wrote down the words. Before I started to work for the ghostwriter.

I realize that there is very little I remember from my life.

I barely remember anything.

I don't know what I did before. I don't know if my childhood was good or bad. I don't know who made an impression on me. I don't know if I have any skills. If anyone has taught me anything. If I've experienced something terrible. If I've been in love. If I've been unhappy.

I only remember what the women have told me.

I only remember what I've heard while listening, while typing.

That is all that's mattered to me. That is the only thing of significance.

If I couldn't listen and type I don't know what I'd be doing. I don't know who I would be.

It's the only thing I know about myself with certainty: that I work for the ghostwriter.

When I wake up, I feel solid.

When I touch my face it no longer gives way.

I look at my hands and see that they're dirty. I place my feet on the floor and take off my shoes. I take off my coat and go to wash my hands in the bathroom. I look at my reflection. I touch my face. I run my hands through my hair, really pulling it from the scalp to make sure I can feel it. I notice that my scalp is a little greasy. My fingers slip over it. I don't remember when I last washed my hair.

That's something I'll deal with later.

I'm happy about my reflection. I'm happy to exist. I haven't disappeared. I'm free. I'm going to go to the ghostwriter's office, I'll give him my pages and we'll drink a little cup of coffee, smoke a little cigarette, and afterward I'll take some time off. The weeks will keep unfolding the way they always do, move forward in their familiar way, and I'll be there. Time will take care of me. I won't change again. I won't become diffuse, I won't lose my balance.

But when I enter the kitchen to get my pages they're not where they're supposed to be. And the cassette player, my cassette player that's always on the kitchen table, is no longer there. And my cassette tapes, I don't see them anywhere. It's as if they were never there. There is not a single trace of them.

I look for them everywhere. I turn the apartment upside down, with mounting horror.

Somebody has stolen my things. Somebody must have broken into my apartment while I was out. My first thought is that I've lost a week's worth of work, but then I think about the transcriptions themselves, the recordings, the women's lives now scattered to the four winds, god knows where.

I call the ghostwriter, but the call won't connect. There's just a beeping noise in my receiver. Nobody picks up. I dial the number again, to no avail. I only have the number for the ghostwriter's office. I don't have his home number. I don't know if he's got a cell phone. He's never given me any other number.

But I have to tell him. I want to.

I try to call him several times, even though I realize that the third or fourth call won't connect, either. I'm distraught. I want to explain what's happened. But nobody picks up.

Finally I put my shoes on, and my coat, and I walk down the stairs, and I walk to the metro. The ground is dirty, slushy. I wait impatiently for the train. When it arrives I get on without letting people get off first, and when the train leaves the station I stand up in the car.

I've got a strange feeling during my ride to the ghostwriter's office, a peculiar feeling, a sense that the other passengers are watching me. They look at me as if they recognize me but hesitate to say hello. As if they know who I am. As if we've met before. I avoid their gazes because I don't recognize them. I don't know them. I get off the train and walk past the laundromat and past the bakery. I walk down the stairs to the ghostwriter's office.

But the door to the office doesn't open when I push it, and when I knock on the door nothing happens. The ghostwriter doesn't come to let me in. I knock again. Then I bang on the door. Then I throw myself at it. There's no way a person inside wouldn't hear me, but nobody comes to open up. I sense, with growing panic, that nobody is there. But I can't know for sure. I remind myself of this: I can't know. I look at the door and try to breathe calmly. Most things in this world have a logical explanation.

I walk onto the street again. I stand there for a moment and look into the distance, ahead to where the street is calm and empty. I listen to the sounds around me. The metro's rattling and the cars. The mopeds. The air smells of exhaust fumes, bread, and detergent. It's a little humid. It's foggy. I can feel the cold on my face and in my bones. A raw, deep cold.

I crouch to peer in through the ghostwriter's window. Inside the little barred square it's pitch-black. The window is covered in dirt. It's all clouded. I get on my knees, lick my fingers, and clean a patch to look inside. I lean forward and put my eye against the patch.

It's very dark in there. It's difficult to see. But I know where everything is supposed to be. I know that the ghostwriter's desk is supposed to stand there, and his weeping fig, his ashtray in black glass, his shelves, his phone, his books and his papers, his coffeepot. The chair he normally sits in and the chair I normally sit in. But when I squint with my eye against the patch, when my eye has gotten used to the complete darkness of the room, I see that nothing is there. The ghostwriter's desk is gone. The room is empty, dusty, and ugly. It is a small, locked, and unremarkable basement room that nobody seems to have used in a very long time. I know this is impossible. I know I was here just a few days ago, and everything was in place then. But I don't know if should trust my memory more than what I see with my own eyes.

I get back on my heels and stand up again. My knees and my hands are dirty.

I take the metro.

I walk up my five flights of stairs.

I wash my hands in the bathroom, and the water that comes off my hands is dark gray.

Then I lie down on top of my bed. The apartment is a complete mess. I've torn my clothes from the closet, my books from the bookcase. The light is gray and matte in here. The windows are dirty. I hear the persistent sound of a dripping faucet, and the sound, from a distance, of the city, which keeps moving.

I don't know what to do.

The ghostwriter is gone, and I'm still here.

NAOMI WAKES UP IN THE MORNING AND HER VOICE IS almost entirely gone. She's tired, too, and her head is heavy. It's the season, Laura says. Everyone is sick this time of year. And you were out in the rain a while ago, weren't you? Yes, Naomi says, that's true. She falls back asleep.

Laura puts out a glass of sparkling water for her.

Then she combs her hair and applies oil. She puts on Naomi's perfume, paints her eyes with Naomi's eyeliner, puts on Naomi's earrings and clothes and boots and coat. On the way to the metro she sticks her hands in her pockets. Walking hurts, but she's getting used to it. In the station kiosk she buys a cup of coffee. She looks at the people who are heading in the same direction or the opposite direction, she looks at their coats, their wool coats, their trench coats, their gloves. A few of them have umbrellas, a few carry a folded issue of CITY under their arms. She looks at the train doors that open, at the people getting off, and once she's on board she watches the doors as they close. She listens to their rattling sound and the slam that follows. When they start to move she listens to the announcements by the female voice, she listens attentively to not miss her station.

She gets off at the radio house. As she enters, she's careful to make her movements familiar, to quell her own fascination for this building she's never visited before, and which looks, she thinks, just like an old vision of the future, modern and aged at once, tall ceilings, concrete and glass, round windows like on a ship. But she can't take it all in, can't look at everything with wonder like someone who's there for the first time, so she makes her eyes slip over the details, the tall ceilings, the wide, curved staircase with the broad banister, the big globe lamps that hang from the ceiling like moons as she displays her pass card and walks up the stairs and onto the elevator and checks, discreetly, the brass sign for the floor she's going to. Every day is the same, she thinks. Yes. This is how it is.

She hangs up her coat. She reads Felix's name on one of the doors. On another, she reads Anne's. She sees the studio farther down the hallway, with its interiors of wood and carpet behind a window. The request hour is still on, and she can hear the muted sounds of the dispatch. They're playing "Morning Mood."

She spends a long time looking for coffee and coffee filters, pulling out every drawer before she finds the filters. Then she adds water and grounds to the coffee machine, but she can't figure out how to operate it. She struggles for a long time, feeling sweat break out across her brow. Hello, gorgeous! she hears a voice exclaim behind her, a booming, beautiful voice she immediately identifies as Felix's, though it's brighter and faster than she's used to from the radio. He's a tall, slim, middle-aged man, not at all what she'd pictured from his voice. He's got bulging eyes and is dressed in a pair of enormous corduroy pants. I always hear you coming, he says, with those boots, ah, you announce your arrival from a mile away in those high-heeled boots, you'd be a useless spy, but I'm always delighted to hear you come, and then, when I see you—always so elegant, you really do dress for the big world! Whenever I lay eyes on you I forget that we're stuck in this big house and its tiny rooms with no windows where everyone is heard but not seen. It brings me joy! Not to mention your fragrance, the way it announces your arrival—ah, it brings me joy! Me, locked up in this gray castle day in and day out, and then there you come with this injection of glamour. What is it? Shiseido? Smells fabulous, whatever it is, very feminine, and just look at your nails, my goodness! Gorgeous! Ah, but look at that, it's almost time for me to head down to the mines. Bring me a cup if you please, when it's done. Are you having trouble? What's with the machine today? I've never been able to understand this stuff, no, I'm not handy at all, not in the least bit, I always say we're lucky we've got you taking care of us. Ah but look here, I know what's missing, this is the issue right here, you forgot to push the magic button, there, I'm told it's something to do with safety, making sure it doesn't stay on overnight, though that doesn't make sense, does it? Are we a little distracted today, my dear? Well, it happens to the best of us!

When Laura comes home, Naomi is waiting for her at the kitchen table. Her voice is almost gone. She's pale, in a cold sweat, and her eyes are swollen and red.

I threw up, she says. And I've got a headache.

Laure touches her forehead. Oh my goodness, you're

burning up, you're boiling hot, she exclaims. You should take a bath. You should have a cup of tea with honey. Have you been drinking water?

She gets the half-full green bottle of sparkling water from the fridge and pours a glass. Naomi watches her.

Where have you been? she asks.

At work, Laura responds, airily.

At work? Naomi repeats. At my job? At the radio?

Yes, Laura replies with a laugh, where else?

Naomi says nothing. She drinks the water. The bubbles pop and fizz in her mouth. She puts the glass down.

You should drink more, Laura says. You should take a bath and then go to bed. You're boiling hot.

Yes, Naomi says. Yes. No. You're right. I'm not feeling well.

She touches her own forehead and cheeks. She drinks.

Did they not realize it wasn't me? she asks.

I don't think so, Laura says.

Naomi considers.

But we don't have the same eye color, she says. And you're a little taller than me.

Yes, Laura says, it's true.

She's quiet for a moment.

Maybe they've never really looked at you, she suggests.

No, Naomi says. Perhaps.

Not the eyes, at least, Laura says.

Naomi says nothing.

It's quite useful, don't you think? Laura says. We can take turns working. Later, when you feel better. One of us can be there, and one of us can take the day off and do whatever she wants.

I like my job, though, Naomi says. I'm happy there. I've got nothing against going there every day.

But what about me? Laura says.

Naomi is silent. She doesn't know how to respond.

I don't want to spend every day all alone at home, Laura says.

No, Naomi says, that makes sense.

It's more fair if we take turns, Laura says.

She looks insistently at Naomi, so insistently that Naomi swallows the words she's got on her tongue, words she can't speak—because they would be too cruel, and because she knows what Laura could say in response. She knows Laura could remind her that it was Naomi who brought Laura home, that it was she who brought her into her life, that it is she who's loved having someone who waits for her at home—so she doesn't respond, Don't you have your own life, but says, instead, after a moment's consideration, Yes, of course. You're right. You're right about that. It's more fair this way.

Laura stamps her ticket and stands up in the metro, predicting the swerves with her thighs, which she braces, and her hand, which tightens its grasp on the leather strap when the train brakes. She pulls her coat tighter and puts her two bare hands into her pockets as she walks up the stairs and into the fresh air. Arriving at the radio house, she ignores the lobby's magnificence and jogs up the steps with one hand on the curved, cool banister after showing her pass card. She takes the elevator up.

On her lunch break she smokes a little cigarette in the radio house's park with Anne. The sky is blue in the pond and the clouds chase across it in big, sharply lit tufts. It's sunny, beautiful out, what a nice day, Anne says, and Laura agrees. Yes, spring is almost here, spring is almost here at last, I can hardly believe it.

On her way home she stops at the supermarket, where she buys a rotisserie chicken, a liter of milk, a bag of apricots, a bottle of sparkling water, and a new box of dye. The plastic bag is thin and heavily weighed down by the groceries, the handle cutting into her naked hand. By the time she's back in the apartment and sets the bag on the floor, it's left red marks.

Naomi comes out of the bedroom as Laura unpacks her groceries in the kitchen. Her eyes are shot through with red. Her hair is matte and unbrushed and there are little zits all around her mouth. Her face is gray. I can't eat that, she says with a look at the chicken, and returns to bed.

Laura puts the milk in the fridge and the apricots in a bowl. A few are bruised and ugly. She tosses those.

She eats half of the chicken. She eats it with her hands, pushing her hands into the bag and pulling the meat straight off the bones with her fingers. She sighs. It's delicious. She sucks the grease from her fingers, which taste lightly of nail polish. She folds the bag and puts it in the fridge.

Then she dyes her hair in the bathroom. She rinses her hair in the tub, and the dark, fake color gurgles in the drain. She dyes her eyebrows. She blinks at the mirror, looking at herself. Her naked shoulders, her nose, her mouth. She wonders how she'll age.

Laura stamps her ticket, she stands up in the train, she gets off at the right stop and displays the pass card with Naomi's name and Naomi's photograph, and then she continues up the stairs and gets in the elevator. Did you read the book? Felix asks when he sees her. What did you think of it? The book? Laura says. Yes, Felix says, that book I gave you, the little red book, about a woman who poisons her husband. I've been so curious to hear your thoughts, really curious. I have to say, it's unlike anything else I've read. I understood almost nothing. Oh, that one, Laura says, yes of course. Now I remember. Yes. It's very strange. Very detailed. Yes, Felix says, incredibly detailed. And with that florid, sweeping style. You thought it was florid? Laura says. I liked the style.

On her way home in the evening, she walks past the Chinese restaurant. The street-facing window is all fogged up, and she can only just make out the red lanterns and the plants in terra-cotta pots inside. She enters. She looks around.

She orders food for take-out. She sits at the bar and rests her chin in her hands while she waits. She'd like to put her cheek on the counter and close her eyes, but she knows that's not done, and the knowledge stops her from doing it. She's tired. It's made her tired to get up early every morning and work all day. Still, she likes being tired in the evenings. She's missed it.

She receives her order in a white plastic bag, and coming home she finds traces of Naomi in the kitchen: a coffee cup, a saucer with eggshells and two apricot kernels. Naomi is in the bedroom, under the covers, in the dark. She's got no makeup on, which makes her eyes look small, Laura thinks, it makes her look stupid, like a stupid shark. Yes, she looks like a shark. The meanness of the thought is surprising. It arrives without effort. She touches Naomi's forehead, which isn't particularly warm. You're burning up, Laura says, you're boiling hot. Come. Drink some water. I got us food.

They eat in front of the TV. They watch an old movie.

A woman has killed her lover.

How do you think she did it? Laura asks. She pokes at the container of rice.

I don't know, Naomi says. It's hard to say.

Maybe it didn't even happen, Laura says.

No, Naomi says, that's true.

We never get to see the body, Laura says. We just assume it's what happened.

Yes, Naomi says, that's true.

They keep watching the movie in silence.

But we see her wash the blood from her hands, Naomi says.

Yes, Laura says, you're right about that.

Laura stamps her ticket, and Naomi is still asleep. She doesn't open her eyes until a few hours later, when her body aches from sleeping so much and her head hurts. She boils an egg. She eats an apricot, tossing the kernel back and forth in her mouth. She forgets to set the egg timer and takes the pot off the stove too early, thinking it's been longer than it has, and when she strikes the egg with her knife to open it, it's slimy, almost uncooked, inside. The yolk hangs from the spoon, the white is almost transparent.

She drinks a cup of coffee.

The weather outside the window is gray and sad, and she's got no choice but to trust that Laura is living her life like she's supposed to.

She goes back to bed.

When she wakes again she puts on the clothes that are closest to the bed, a button-down and a pair of pants. The clothes are soft and smell a little musty. She puts on perfume. Though she's heavy, tired, and sleepy she feels she needs to go outside. She goes outside and walks, with no other goal than having something to do, and the weather is still dreary. There's a drizzle in the air and she checks for her gloves in her pockets but they're not there, so she just pushes her hands deeper into the pockets to warm up. Her hands feel dry and cracked against the lining. She walks along the canal, but the path is muddy and she doesn't want to ruin her shoes. She walks up to the street and continues on the sidewalk, peering into the cafés when she walks past them, into the doors of the buildings. She walks past a building where someone has taped up several flyers, amateurishly made, on simple, thin printer paper. A woman who lives on the block has disappeared and there's a photograph, the last time she was seen, taken by a surveillance camera.

Naomi thinks to herself that the disappeared woman has people in her life who care about her.

Naomi thinks to herself that in the past, before Laura entered her life, she used to be alone, but lately, even though there are two of them now, Laura's presence has made her feel lonelier than before. She doesn't feel free. She feels constantly watched. And she feels, at the same time, strangely abandoned. She tries to catch this feeling as she walks, slowly, down the street. She used to be alone, yes, but she used to feel like herself. Now it feels as if somebody has taken something from her.

Laura goes to the swimming pool after work and gets home late, tired and distracted, and at night she falls asleep before Naomi.

You should have seen me! You should have seen me! You should have seen me when I was young! I had big, clear eyes, and my hair was dark like ebony! And I had the most unusual side gig: I worked as a body double! When an actress didn't want to be naked on screen, that's when I came in! You'd see her face in the film, but it was my body! I remember I went to see one of those movies in the theater, several years after it had first premiered, with...well, why did they show it in the theater, several years later? Why was that? It wasn't exactly quality cinema, these films. I remember that much. No, it was a lot of blood and violence, no finesse at all...I remember that much...but why they were showing it at that point, I can't remember for the life of me. In any case we went to see it in the theater. And my friends, my...the people I went with...they felt it was well done, they said, really well done—they wouldn't have known it was two different people if I hadn't told them—they couldn't recognize me, they said—they wouldn't have been able to recognize me from just looking at the body, without seeing the face—they were impressed, impressed by the craft—but as far as I was concerned, no! To me—to me it was absolutely, entirely obvious! It was a strange feeling—I thought it was so obvious, and really awkward, this clear sense that it was *two* people, and that it was my body in the frame, my body, but, so to speak, headless...

THE NEXT DAY I RETURN TO THE GHOSTWRITER'S OFFICE, but he's still gone. The following day I go to his office again, but he's still gone. He is still gone when I get to his office on the third day, and after that I wait a few days to go back, as if trying to trick someone.

There is a logic to my behavior, but I don't seek it.

On the days I don't go to his office I'm able to convince myself that it's all in my head. Perhaps I was mistaken. I remember the office as unfurnished, abandoned, with the lights off, but I could be mistaken. I could be mistaken. I've never quite trusted my memory fully.

On the days that I don't go to his office, I clean my apartment. I put everything back in order that I tore down while looking for my pages, the cassette tapes, and the tape player. I make the apartment look nice. I wipe down the radio, which is dusty, and I listen to music. I take the coins from the stoneware bowl by the door and sort them in stacks, the smallest copper coins in one stack, the bigger copper coins in one stack, the silver coins in one stack, and then, when I know exactly how much they amount to, I go to Rigardi with my coins and order an espresso and a sparkling water. I've got the exact sum for this order. I counted the coins. Even though I've counted them, the woman who takes my coins also wants to count them, and this takes a long while. While she counts I look out the window with my chin in my hands. She's lit a candle on the bar and its flame flickers. It's getting dark, all blue outside the window, though it's only afternoon.

She gives me my coffee and my water. I'm the only customer at Rigardi. The woman who works there is chewing gum and flipping through a magazine. I drink my coffee and think to myself that I should head home soon and get to transcribing. Then I remember, with a pang of despair, that I won't be doing that at all. But there's a glimmer of hope in that pang, too. I haven't given up. I'm not yet convinced that the ghostwriter has really vanished.

I know there are things I don't know about him, things I will never understand.

In fact, I know almost nothing about him.

I wonder what's going to happen to the women if he really and truly has vanished.

Who is going to write the story of their lives now? I wonder where the books he was writing, the stories he hadn't yet finished, have gone. I wonder if he took them when he disappeared. I wonder if they were stolen. I wonder if my tapes and my cassette player and my pages were stolen. I wonder who could want to steal them, and who could have known of their existence. I've never told anyone about my work. It's always been between me and the ghostwriter. It's always been between us. Our private concern. And the women's.

I drink a little water to chase the bitter coffee taste from my tongue, keeping the water in my mouth for a few seconds. The bubbles dance and pop against the roof of my mouth. I swallow and step into the chilly outdoors.

One day I get up early and take the metro. It's dark when I leave, and inside the train the light is yellow, almost orange, a light that makes the faces look gray and their eyes black. I travel to the ghostwriter's office. On the platform I buy a coffee in the kiosk. I open a sachet of sugar and stir it into the hot coffee. I do this to slow down time. Then it strikes me that I normally buy a coffee only after I've seen the ghostwriter. Maybe it's bad luck that I did it before going to the office this time.

I walk past the laundromat and the bakery as usual, and I know that my hope is a fantasy, something I attempt but don't manage to conjure. And the ghostwriter's window is, just as I knew in my heart of hearts and soul of souls, black. And when I kneel in front of the window and look inside, everything looks just like it did last time. It looks as if the office hasn't been used in a very long time. There is not a single trace of the ghostwriter there. I don't know where else I could look for him. I don't know where he lives. I don't know anyone who's met him. I don't know his name. I couldn't prove to anyone that he's existed.

I go back home.

I lie down on my bed with my hands folded over my belly, and I look at the ceiling.

I think about how I feel solid again, about how I no longer feel like I'm disappearing. But it's useless to be solid now. It's useless to be solid when I'm alone. I don't know what to do with myself. With my solid body. With my clear thoughts.

I think to myself that I've lost everything that made my life meaningful.

I've got a bit of money, but not a lot. I need a job, but I don't know what. I know nothing other than listening and typing. I don't know how to go about getting a job like that.

I don't remember anything other than my job for the ghostwriter.

I have to fill my days with something.

I go to Submondo, I watch the movies again and again. Sometimes I nod off in my seat. It feels good to doze, slouched in the darkness of the theater. I go to Rigardi and drink two cups of coffee. They only charge for the first cup. I sit at the bar, watching as the café fills with people. Sometimes I go to the department store, take the escalators to the top of the building, and sit down in the café. I listen to the din rising from the floors below and the tables around me. I drink a little cup of coffee and eat a little chocolate praline that doesn't cost me anything. Persipan.

It gets dark earlier and earlier. The darkness makes me feel a little strange. It feels as if it's the middle of the night when it's only the afternoon.

I understand that I have to make a new life for myself. I don't want to. I have no wish for a new life. I liked my old one. But I can't keep living the way I do. I can see that myself. I see it, reluctantly. It feels as if I have a doppelgänger. As if there were two of me. It feels as if my life has moved on without me, and I have no other choice but to move on, too.

I need to become somebody else.

I spend a long time considering how to go about it,

who I would like to become. I ride the metro back and forth, looking at the other passengers. Sometimes I find someone to trail for a little while. Someone who interests me. But I almost always tire of it.

I go to Rigardi and look at people. I sit there and read my magazine.

I begin to get rid of my belongings. I need money.

First I sell my radio. I don't get much for it. Then I sell my books, my china, my kitchen table and my chairs, the stoneware bowl where I put my keys and my coins. The stoneware bowl turns out to be the most valuable item. I keep my computer for as long as I can, but finally I sell that, too.

Soon I won't own anything other than the clothes on my body. And the lipstick. And my secret transcription.

It's the only keepsake from my life with the ghostwriter. It's my only proof.

I go to the department store, which is decorated for Christmas with artificial pine, artificial holly, lanterns, and red ribbons. I take a seat at one of the tables in the café, with my coat still on.

Then, on the escalator, I see a woman in a coat similar to mine. Almost identical. I recognize her. I have seen her. I saw her with the ghostwriter. The last time I met with him. I didn't see her face that time, but I know it's her when she comes up the escalator, when her dark eyes scan the café, looking, I assume, for somewhere to sit.

She's attractive. She's got dark, very shiny hair. I wonder how it can be so shiny.

She takes her gloves off and puts them in her pocket,

then takes her coat off and sits down at a table on the other side of the café. She drinks a cup of coffee. She doesn't touch the praline that's included in the price.

After she stands up, pays, puts on the coat again, and rides down the escalator, I discreetly walk up to her table and steal her untouched praline.

After that day I see her at the department store café several times.

It never looks like she's been shopping. She always drinks a little cup of coffee that she stirs the contents of a small, pale-blue sachet of sweetener into. She always comes alone.

I don't think she's ever noticed me.

One day, after she pays for her coffee, puts on her coat, and takes the escalator down, I follow her. I follow her from the department store. She walks along the canal, and I walk next to her, where she doesn't see me, on the sidewalk. The road separates us, and every time a car drives by I worry I'll lose sight of her, but then I see her again, on the other side.

She crosses one of the bridges. I follow.

She unlocks a door and walks in.

I linger across the street and watch the lights come on in the stairwell. I soon get cold, so I leave.

She lives not far from me. I commit the route to memory.

I think about how to approach her. I think about how I can get her to notice me.

I see her again at the department store and follow her when she leaves.

She doesn't go home. She goes to a pool and swims.

I go inside and sit down at the pool cafeteria. I drink a little cup of coffee. It doesn't taste very good. The cafeteria smells strongly of chlorine. The smell gives me a headache, and I leave. It's not the right place. Not the right time. I don't know what to say to her. I don't know how to make her notice me.

One day at the department store café, I see her arrive. I watch her hang up her coat, like she always does. I watch her order her coffee, like she always does.

While she talks to the waiter I go up to the hook where she's hung her coat. I hang my own coat on top of hers.

I want to tell you. I'm going to. I just don't know where to begin. I just need a moment, a moment to collect myself, to find the right words. Then I'll tell you.

THE BODY LOOKS ODDLY YOUNG, NAOMI THINKS AS SHE sinks deeper into her seat in the twenty-four-hour movie theater. They show the same film several times, again and again. When it ends there's a pause for a few seconds, a black square before it begins anew. She got there somewhere in the middle and she's seen how it ends—now she learns how it begins. It's a shot of a naked woman, a naked woman brushing her own blond, short hair in front of a full-length mirror, and the body, Naomi thinks, doesn't match her face. She's got a middle-aged woman's face, but the body looks like it belongs to a twenty-year-old. Naomi is preoccupied by this body in the mirror. She looks at the woman's stomach, her breasts, her bright-pink nipples, her firm arms, the smooth hand that holds the brush. Nobody brushes their hair that way, Naomi thinks. She sinks even farther into her seat. She's sleepy, even though it's the middle of the day.

She watches the film up until the scene that was playing when she got to the theater and then stays a few additional minutes before she gets up and goes outside.

The air outside Submondo is lukewarm. She stands in place on the sidewalk to get acclimatized to the gray, tepid daylight, breathing for a moment while she thinks about where to go. Eventually she sets off at random. She enters a kiosk and buys a little cup of coffee. Back on the street again she takes a sip and burns her tongue, and because the lid isn't properly fastened she spills coffee on her chest and stains her coat. She tries to wipe it with her hand. She shouldn't be wearing this coat, it's too warm for the time of year. She pauses in front of the window of an antiques store, looking at the things on display—a table in marble and glass, agate grapes, a Jugendstil vase—and looking, in the reflection, at the stain the coffee's left on her coat, and as she scrutinizes the stain, her gaze wanders upward and she looks, appalled, at her own face, realizing with a terrible feeling that she doesn't look like herself. She doesn't look the way she normally looks. Her face looks swollen and wan and she's not worn makeup in forever. She can't see the point when she barely goes out anyway, when nobody is looking at her. There's something wrong, she feels, with her stamina. It's as if somebody is sucking out all her energy. She can't be bothered to wash her face. She can't be bothered to care for her nails, cut them and file them. They're chipped and dirty.

I've been sick, she thinks in an attempt to soothe herself. It's not permanent. No, there's no reason to worry, no reason to despair. And in any case what would it matter anyway if it were permanent, if she were to be met by this sight every time she looked into a mirror, this face she doesn't recognize, doesn't want to claim. If she were forever ugly. It wouldn't be a disaster. It wouldn't be the end of the world. This is not all she is.

She turns back home. She takes the path along the canal. She puts her hands in her pockets and the lining is slippery.

Laura must have taken the wrong coat when she left this morning. And now Naomi has taken Laura's.

She gets home. She washes her hair. She puts oil in her hands to apply it to her hair and notices that the bottle is almost empty.

She's bored. Laura won't be back from the radio house for several hours yet.

She dials the number for Karol and Larissa's home phone and listens as it rings. Nobody picks up and she doesn't leave a message, but shortly after she hangs up Karol calls her. I couldn't get to the phone in time, he says, but I'm so glad you called, it's nice to hear your voice. It's as if you'd read my thoughts. I really needed a distraction. What's this voice, though, you poor thing, you sound different, has something happened? Did you get sick again, you poor thing? I hope we didn't give you something? No, Naomi says, that seems unlikely. Well, Karol says, stranger things have happened. Thanks for coming over the other day. I should be the one thanking you, Naomi says. Lou was so happy about the present, Karol says, perfect choice, really a great present. Present? Naomi says. Did we bring Lou a present? I don't think we brought Lou anything?

Karol laughs, but his laughter is defensive and joyless, and it makes Naomi nervous. Sure you did, he says, of course, you did bring a present. I did? Naomi says. Karol is silent on the other end of the line. This is making me wonder who I'm really talking to, he says, finally. Is that you, Naomi? Yes, Naomi says, of course it's me. You can see the caller ID, who else would it be?

Karol is silent again, he's silent for so long that Naomi finally asks if he's still there. Yes, he says, I'm still here. But why are you calling me from home this time of day? Shouldn't you be at work? I left early, Naomi says. It's

Friday, Karol says, and Naomi remembers, yes, it's Friday, which means the concert, which means it's going to be even longer until Laura comes home, and the thought of the long, lonely evening makes her feel deep despair; so does Karol's tone of voice, his suddenly distant, cold voice. Yes, Naomi says, but I went home early because I felt a little sick. Okay, Karol says. I hope you feel better soon. I have to go, sorry.

He hangs up without another word, and Naomi looks at the mute receiver in her hand.

She hangs up, too.

Then she waits for Laura to come home.

She sits in the armchair, in the dark.

When it's almost midnight she hears the sound of the doorknob being pushed down, and then she sees the contours of Laura entering and closing the door behind her, very carefully, as if she's trying not to wake Naomi. She stops right inside the threshold and stands there in the dark without moving, facing Naomi's direction but without, it seems, being able to see her.

Hello? she says, at last. Is anybody there?

I'm here, Naomi says and stands up from the armchair. Laura brings her hand to her heart, and the gesture, how theatrical it is, irritates Naomi. I didn't see you, Laura says, and she takes off her coat. She smells of chilly evening when she comes to embrace Naomi, putting a cool cheek against hers. She takes Naomi's hands and looks into her eyes, and Naomi looks into Laura's eyes, into Laura's pale eyes, those still very pale eyes that are not at all dark like her own, and suddenly she wants to gouge out those pale, staring eyes that look like the eyes of a fish or a blind person, those unnaturally pale eyes that are so obviously not her eyes, something anybody should be able to see, anybody who knows her well, and anger rises in her, a despairing anger she doesn't know what to do with.

Is she the only person who sees Laura's eyes? Does nobody else notice?

Did you go to visit Lou and Karol without me? Naomi asks. The question wells up and out of her, like her anger. She hadn't planned to ask and when she does she hates how it sounds, jealous and hysterical and grudging.

Laura shakes her head, and Naomi detects no feeling in her eyes at all. No shock, no shame at the question. Her hands, which are still holding Naomi's, are limp.

Did you give Lou a present? she asks. I was on the phone with Karol and he thanked me for the present, but I have no memory of any present. I have no memory of going to visit them after we went together. Did you? Did you see them without me?

Laura just shakes her head, and her passivity, that empty gaze, nearly makes Naomi crazy.

You can do it at the radio, Naomi says, I'm okay with that, we agreed on it, we discussed it, it's only fair. And I don't care if the neighbors confuse us, or strangers in the city. But you can't pretend to be me with my friends. That's creepy. Do you understand? It's strange to behave like that. Do you understand?

Laura drops Naomi's hands and keeps looking at her with those empty, blank, pale eyes. It makes Naomi ill at ease, and suddenly she's afraid of going too far. Afraid that something might happen if she keeps on insisting. Laura's silence makes her doubt herself.

Say something, she says.

I promise I haven't gone to see your friends, Laura says, and her voice is just a brittle whisper. She clears her throat. Perhaps, she says, carefully, you went and forgot about it?

Laura's cautious, coaxing tone repulses Naomi. And even though she knows exactly what she's done this week and even the week before, even though she could swear that she's definitely not seen her friends, though she could take an oath on it, Laura's question makes a trickle of doubt pulse through her veins. So she nods. Yes, she says. I'm sorry. Maybe you're right. Maybe I forgot.

Laura takes Naomi's hands again and says, Let's do something fun tomorrow.

It's the kind of day that smells of dust from newly swept sidewalks, a dry and sunny day, and they walk to the square, to the market, identically dressed, arm in arm, in their coats and their sunglasses. The market has flowers in yellow and white buckets, irises, roses, lilies, gerberas, baby's breath, tulips, and branches of apple blossoms, cherry blossoms, but not—Naomi looks for them—peach blossoms. There are vegetables and jars of honey. There are folding tables with blankets and all sorts of things displayed for sale: pots, tableware and lamps, paintings, ornaments, kitsch, porcelain figurines, embroidery, napkins and towels, medallions and coins and stamps, books, toys, clothes, photographs. Laura opens a Bible and deciphers the dedication: a confirmation gift, 1914.

They've not been out together in a long while and Naomi is ready for people to stare at them, ready for others to think it's strange to see them walking like this, arm in arm with the same haircuts and the same clothes and their black sunglasses, but nobody looks at them, nobody does a double take, nobody seems to notice them at all and she realizes that it's making her a little disappointed.

She lets go of Laura's arm and wanders through the market alone. One table has an embroidered white linen cloth for sale, and on top of it are drinking glasses of all kinds, smooth glasses, thin glasses etched with grapes and grape leaves, shot glasses, liqueur glasses, wineglasses, water glasses, green glass rummers, cocktail glasses, blue glass, gray glass. Naomi touches the glasses, lifts them and clinks them lightly against each other to hear what kind of sound they make, if it's a ringing sound or a mute sound, and she holds up a glass with a thin, etched band in the sunlight, puts it down, and touches a set of twelve little crystal punch cups arranged in two teetering stacks. She digs through a box of old photographs, very old photos, black-and-white photos and studio photographs, families in their Sunday best, old men, young children, women with serious faces, serious hair. She buys a vase, copper green with a pattern in relief, haggling to reduce an already cheap price to almost nothing. She receives it wrapped in thick newsprint, and a piece of tape runs over a thick, black word: MURDER!

She heads to a table that's overfull and cluttered with all manner of objects, radios, coffee cups with wooden saucers, a red clay teapot, a stoneware bowl, a cassette player, key rings, Duralex glasses, and ashtrays. Amid the detritus on the table is a cardboard box. It's a regular shoebox, a tattered old box closed with tape, the same kind of rough masking tape used on the newsprint around the vase Naomi holds in her arms. The vendor is nearby, smoking and drinking coffee from a brown paper cup. He peers at her searchingly.

You look the same, he says. Naomi turns to him. Pardon? she says. You look the same, he repeats. You and your friend. He nods at Laura, who is browsing leisurely a few tables off, looking maybe a little bored, her hands in her pockets. Yes, Naomi says with a polite smile. You're right.

She picks up the cassette player and looks at it from every angle. Then she sets it down again. She's about to move on when Laura comes up to them. The vendor looks at her and pulls on his cigarette. She, too, lifts up the cassette player. She weighs it in her hands.

Who did all these things belong to? she asks.

Different people, he responds, curtly.

Where do they come from? she asks.

Estate sales, he responds.

Is that all you know? she asks.

Yup, he responds. That's all I know.

Are you sure that all this belonged to people who are dead? she asks.

I know that much, he says.

He flings his cigarette on the ground and blows on his coffee. Laura puts the cassette player down again. She points at the box in the center of the table.

What's in the box? she asks the vendor.

Can't tell you, he responds.

Why not? Naomi asks.

The vendor just shakes his head.

I can't, he says. If you want to open the box you'll have to buy it.

We'll buy it, Laura says.

Naomi pays with a banknote. No change.

They head home, but before they leave the market Naomi stops by the flower stalls on the edge of the square. She wants something to put in her new vase. She presses the vase to her chest while she handles the flowers, lifting them from the pails. Water drips from the stems. Laura cradles the box in her arms. She's sweating. Her face is damp. Her sunglasses keep slipping down her nose. She adjusts them and looks across the square and toward the bald vendor and his table with the cassette player, the teapot, the stoneware bowl, and the radio, but she no longer sees his table, and when she scans the market she doesn't see the vendor anywhere, either, he's nowhere, nowhere at all. Naomi pays for a bouquet of irises, yellow and purple. She uses a banknote and gets her change.

Naomi wants to open the box with a knife, but Laura prefers to carefully strip off the masking tape. It's really glued to the box, in multiple layers. Meanwhile Naomi makes a sharp cut across the green stem of the irises, and she removes the newsprint around the vase, balls it up and discards it, then puts the flowers in water. She puts the knife down on the counter and the vase on the table.

Naomi is done and Laura is still working. She labors with great focus. She's still wearing her coat and she's pushed the sunglasses up on her forehead. Naomi turns on the radio and sits down next to Laura.

Finally she unpeels the last piece of tape. They open the box together. It's full of cassette tapes.

Laura looks at Naomi.

Naomi takes one of the tapes and looks to see if there's anything written on it, but it has no label. She takes another tape, and that one doesn't have a label, either.

I've got nothing to play them with, she says. We should have bought that cassette player.

They're probably both a little disappointed by the box's contents, Naomi thinks. The tight seal and the vendor's insistence that they needed to buy it to know what was inside had promised a bigger secret.

Laura stands up and puts her sunglasses on the table. She goes to the hall to hang her coat up and returns to the kitchen. She asks if Naomi wants a glass of water. Yes, Naomi says, I'd love one. Laura takes the green bottle of sparkling water from the fridge, pours a glass, and hands it to Naomi. Don't you want to split it? she asks. Oh, no, Laura says, no, it's just water, after all. Tap water is good enough for me.

She pours herself a glass and drinks it, still standing at the sink. Naomi drinks from her glass. The bubbles crackle on her tongue and against the roof of her mouth.

She looks at her hands and finds that they're all dirty, soiled from touching the newsprint the vase was wrapped in. She goes to the bathroom to wash them. She washes them for a long time. The water turns dark gray under the tap. She washes her hands for a very long time and the water continues to be dark gray, it's dark gray for a very long time. She scrubs underneath her nails, the nails with chipped mother-of-pearl varnish. The soap bar is white and oval. It slips from her hands and she drops it on the floor, and when she picks it up there's a long strand of hair stuck to it. She pulls the hair off and flushes it down the drain. Then she rinses the soap clean and puts it on the edge of the sink. She rinses her hands and dries them. She looks at her palms. They're red.

She checks her own reflection. She looks sickly and pale. She touches her face, her cheeks. She's got a feeling that they're spongy, sort of porous. She adjusts her hair. The viscous, sticky oil has trickled down behind her ears and down her neck, and now it's found its way inside the collar of her sweater. Her temples are sweaty, and her hairline, too. She's never thought the oil smelled before, but suddenly she notices a scent. It hits her with full force, rich and hard to place, fusty and sweet. Is it even a scent, or more of a smell? A stench? Has it gone rancid? Something, she feels, smells rotten. She swallows a few times, but her throat is still dry.

She walks into the kitchen, where the box of cassette tapes is on the table, and so is the vase with the flowers and her empty water glass, and there's a rerun on the radio. Gounod. She recognizes the music. She can hear Felix's rumbling voice: Amour, ranime mon courage. This is exactly his kind of music.

But Laura is not in the kitchen, and her sunglasses are not on the table, and only one coat is hanging in the hall.

Naomi looks for her in the bedroom, and then she goes back into the bathroom and looks for her there, but Laura is nowhere. She calls her name but receives no answer. She returns to the kitchen. She looks at the table again, the vase with the flowers, her own empty water glass, the box with the cassette tapes and the sink with Laura's water glass, which has a slight, brown, half-moon mark from her lipstick at the top. The empty sink. Sun fills the kitchen. She should clean the windows.

Laura has left, Naomi thinks. She must have left, gone without a sound while I was washing my hands.

She puts her coat on and leaves the apartment, she walks down the stairs and out onto the street and she looks to the right and to the left but she doesn't see Laura anywhere. She starts walking toward the metro. Jogging down the stairs she nearly stumbles, but she catches the handrail at the last moment, finding her balance. She hears, through the walls, the sound of a busker on the accordion. Lambada. The music echoes between the station's tiles. There is a smell of coffee and urine. She stamps her ticket, BANG, and the sound explodes in her skull. She stands up as the train moves, she holds on to a leather strap, but before she's even traveled one stop and arrived at the old aboveground wrought-iron station she has to sit down. She sinks onto a seat. She has to lean her forehead against the window. She's got a cold sweat. She smells her own unwashed body and old clothes, and when she looks at the reflections of the other passengers, when she looks at their faces, she's got the sense that they're looking at her, too, but not with warmth. She's got the sense that they're looking at her as if they recognize her, though she doesn't recognize them. She slips her hands into her pockets, and the cool, slippery lining burns against her scoured skin. She feels Laura's lipstick, which is there, with the heavy ridged tube. She squeezes the lipstick in her pocket. It's the wrong coat. Laura has taken the wrong coat again. But this can be fixed. When she finds Laura she's going to set it right.

The people sitting closest to her move. One by one they get off the train, and soon she's alone in the car with her forehead against the window, and the train keeps moving. They travel through the darkness, through the underground.

The image is of a metro car, a fairly timeless image. Seats in artificial blue leather, silver-colored stanchions, leather straps. The light is saturated, greenish. The doors close. This is the final image. This is the final image.